THE RIDEALONG

by

Michaelbrent Collings

**website: http://www.michaelbrentcollings.com
email: info@michaelbrentcollings.com**

cover and interior art elements © Aleshyn_Andrei and spixel
used under license from Shutterstock.com
cover design by Michaelbrent Collings

For more information on Michaelbrent's books, including specials and sales; and for info about signings, appearances, and media,

**check out his webpage,
Like his Facebook fanpage**
or
Follow him on Twitter.

DEDICATION

To...

Tonn Peterson, because he likes to be scared,
and he plays hooky sometimes,

Shane Langton, who drove me around,
and probably showed me more than he wanted,

and to Laura, FTAAE.

Contents

PART ONE:

A DREAM IS A DREAM
YOUR HEART MAKES

June 30
PD Property Receipt – Evidence
Case # IA15-6-3086
Rec'd: 6/29
Investigating Unit: IA/Homicide

JOURNAL
DAY ONE

Dad came home and talked to me and told me everything.

Wait, that's too late in the story.

I guess I should start with: I think it's weird that I'm starting a journal. Dad always said I should have one. Said it was "like a best friend... only one you never have to lie to." He always said that with his dumb grin, like he's telling the funniest joke ever only he knows it's not funny at all and he just doesn't care.

But I care now. I'm writing this so I don't have to lie. Because I'm scared, and I don't want Dad to know.

Dad came home and talked to me.

He told me everything.

I wish he hadn't. Because now it's all I think about, all I know. Sometimes I close my eyes and it's not like I'm there, it's like it's all I <u>am</u>.

So now we aren't talking much. Dad talks to <u>me</u> all the time. Like he's afraid he's going to lose me the way he did Mom. But I don't talk back. I can't. What if he guesses how scared I am, how much he changed me that day?

I think that would kill him.

So I won't lie. I won't tell him.

Ha. Now <u>that's</u> the lie.

1

I am in someone else's body.

There are four other cops.

Tim Knight, a tall guy who looks like a brick with angry eyes. But when he smiles the anger disappears and he looks like a kid at Disneyland.

Ben Zevahk, short and round and looks soft but once he invited a 'banger to punch him in the stomach and when the kid took the shot it broke his wrist.

Jedediah Voss, who insists on being called "Jedediah," and not "Jed" and every time he makes a big deal he laughs like it's funny, but he's a prick and a jackass and everyone knows it.

Steve Linde. My partner. Smiling and laughing all the time. Too much for a cop, like he's practicing to be a circus clown when he retires.

And me. Don't forget me. I'm there. I'm the fifth cop on the scene, even though I'm not really me, I'm someone else. I'm a cop here, in this place, but a part of me knows that this is not reality. Even though I'm caught in this now, in this place, I know that this isn't me isn't me *can't be me.*

Glass breaks. I hear the quiet creak of leather, the sounds my equipment makes as it rubs against my waist. Then all that is lost in the noise of gunshots. Bursts from a fully automatic weapon.

Knight screams: "Jesus!"

Zevahk: "Where's he at?"

Another burst of gunfire and Linde starts screaming. Hit. I can't tell how bad – he was crouched on the other side of the patrol car we share. Only a few feet away, but his screams sound so far, and I can't see him from where I huddle and hide.

I should go to him.

I should go to them.

I make a move. Knight darts out and grabs me. Stops me.

"They'll die!" My voice – so deep, so gruff –

(*so not me this isn't me this can't be me who is this if it isn't me?*)

– cracks as I scream, "They'll die!"

"They're dead already!"

The words are a slap in the face. They're horrible. They're painful.

They're true.

There are two bodies in the street between us and the shooter. One is also holding a gun. A righteous kill.

The other one holds no gun. Holds nothing but some books, maybe a phone in a death-clenched hand. A kid. The same age as –

Don't go there. Don't think that. Get the job done.

I'm here. I'm now. I can't think of anything else. If I waste brain space on what's already been lost today, then I'll be making sure we lose even more.

Besides... what if they're not dead? Linde is still screaming, my partner is still alive. So maybe the kid is, too. Maybe we can save –

More shots cut through my hope.

Then the sounds of Linde, still screaming. High-pitched shrieks that drill into my mind, shattering my thoughts.

It's so loud, good God, so loud.

Knight shouts, "We've gotta take this guy!"

Zevahk laughs. An angry sound. "Ya think?"

"How long until backup gets here?" That's me. My voice sounds faraway. Not just like it's someone else, but like it's a whole other life, a whole other reality. An *un*me.

Knight gapes at me. He and Zevahk are crouched behind open doors of their patrol car. They've been partners forever. Best friends and brothers the way only cops can be.

"Are you kidding me, you think we're gonna –?" Knight begins.

Another flurry of shots cuts him off.

Linde is still screaming, but the screams are getting quieter. Bleeding away as he bleeds out.

"On three! We take him on three!" Not sure whether that was Knight or Zevahk or Voss. Not Linde. My partner is still screaming, no words, just wordless pain.

Everything's bleeding together. Just like Linde is bleeding out, like the blood all over the kid in the street. Blood everywhere.

"On three!" That was Zevahk.

"One."

I want to scream, No! Wait!

"Two!"

What's going on? Why can't I talk?

Because this isn't me. It's a dream. It's happening to someone else.

I'm not really here.

"THREE!"

My legs push up on their own. I don't control them, I don't control *anything*. I'm here but I'm not me. In this place I am just an observer, just a watcher. I cannot act, I can only follow along with what must happen.

Guns fire. The rapid-fire pounding of a full-auto rifle. The irregular pummeling of semi-automatics being shot as fast as fingers can pull the triggers.

So loud. So loud, I can't think.

Something punches me in the shoulder. I wonder who did that. Everything's bleeding together. Bleeding –

(*like Voss, like the kid in the street, like the now of it all*)

– and then bled and done. The world loses its color.

The shooting has stopped.

I'm falling.

Shot. I was shot.

No. Not me. Someone else.

It all happened in seconds.

I'm dying.

Not me. Not....

So fast. But lives changed. Lives ended.

Blood in the street.

I hear a voice. "You killed my baby!" It's torn with grief, with rage, with pain. "I'll kill you! I'll kill you all!"

Then my long fall finally ends. A long laydown across asphalt that for some reason feels soft. So soft. So wet. Bloody.

It all bleeds together. Bleeds to black.

"I'll kill you all!"

It's the last thing I hear before...

2

... I wake up and I'm me again.

For a second I can't understand where I am. Where the bright sun went, the hot asphalt under me and the blood all around.

I'm on a bed. Not as soft as that final pillow the street made for the person I was in my dream, but certainly more friendly. Still, it doesn't seem right. For a moment this doesn't seem like the place I should be.

I don't belong here.

The dream is still a part of me. Still something that insists on its reality. I look around my bedroom: the bedroom of a teenage girl. Posters, pictures of friends, the desk that Dad gave me so I could do schoolwork on – a joke since I do all my schoolwork on the kitchen table. Every item I see shoves the dream back a little bit. Slices bits of it off until it retreats and becomes, not reality, but nightmare. Not memory, but merely fear.

As soon as I think that, Dad's voice moves into the room. He's seemed to be at my elbow since the shooting, since the event that spun me into the constant nightmare.

(*Five cops went in. Two made it out fine, but my dad and another cop came out shot. A third came out dead. Protect and serve, ain't it a hoot!*)

"The dream again?" His voice is calm. Low. The voice of the guy who took on double duties with no complaint when Mom died. Who rocked me all night long when my eardrum burst as a seven-year-old. Who would do anything for me.

That voice pushes the nightmare back a bit more. It always does. But at the same time, I know that the voice is the *source* of the nightmare.

Because what if I had lost him? What if he had gone away that day... and never come back?

I don't say that. It would be too real if I did. The nightmare would come back, and this time it wouldn't be a dream, it would by my reality.

Instead: "It's like I was there with you, Dad."

I sense him trying to smile. "I should never have –"

I know how he's going to finish the sentence. We've always been close. Closer now than ever.

I should never have let you in on this.

I should never have told you.

I should never have let you grow up.

None of that matters. None of it changes what happened. What I feel now. How afraid I am.

"I don't want you to go back," I say. And I finally look at him. He's leaning on my doorjamb, just like I knew he would be. Dressed in the same thing he always wears: jeans, t-shirt, cross-trainers. Hunt Leigh Knight is a man of simple tastes. Not the smartest bulb in the marquee of life, as he always says. But he's mine. I couldn't stand losing him.

But that shootout...

He's leaning against his left shoulder. As if to prove it's all right. As if to prove the bullet hole is completely healed, there's nothing to worry about. Good as new, let's move on.

"I don't want you to go back," I say again.

His smile gets strained. Maybe it's because his shoulder hurts.

"Nothing good happens without work," he says. "No pain no gain."

I don't think that's funny. And I don't know if I can handle him not being around today.

Thirty-one days ago my father stumbled into a drug bust gone bad. He was shot. One of his brothers – his partner, Steve Linde – was shot and killed. Another was shot and just got out of the hospital.

Three others were killed in the shootout as well.

Dad could have died. Almost did.

And today is going to be his first day back since the shooting.

3

We're on our way out the door when the phone rings. I don't know why we even have a landline – Dad and I both have cells, and it seems weird for him to toss fifty bucks a month at the phone company for the privilege of maybe six phone calls.

Though there were a lot more these last few weeks. Condolences, concerns.

"Can you get that?" Dad says.

There's a phone on the little table in the entry. I pick it up. "Latham drug den, where we serve your crack, how may I help you?" I say. Dad laughs nearby, which means I'll get an earful about answering the phone nicely. But he'll scold me while he smiles. And that's cool. Dad tries to be what he thinks of as "a good father" wrapped up in "a good mother," but he's never kept it a secret that he doesn't feel up to either task. And I think me saying stupid crap on the phone kinda reassures him. Like he's catching me at little things, so he doesn't have to worry about big ones.

"Can we talk?"

For some reason my stomach falls out through my knees. It used to be when Liam called my stomach turned in happy knots. Now I just feel sick.

Everything's changed.

Maybe this is what growing up feels like.

"Now's not a good time."

"Please, I just want to… I need to talk to you –"

"Liam, I can't. I'm on my way out. Maybe –"

"It has to be *now!*"

The shout catches me off guard. Shuts me up for a few seconds. I suddenly feel like I'm back in that dream. "I'm sorry about what happened," he says. "I'm so, so sorry." He sounds like he's crying now. *Crying.* "I just… I need to talk to you. I feel like you're the only one I can trust."

What's going on?

The dream feeling. The feeling like I'm somewhere else, someone and some*when* else – it's so strong I'm spinning.

"I'll talk to you later," I say.

He sounds like he's going to keep on going. And I don't want to hear whatever he's going to say. He'll ask why we're not talking, what happened, why we stopped going out. Whatever it is, I don't want to answer.

I don't really *know* the answer.

Everything's changed.

"Gotta go," I say again.

"No, I don't – I can't believe what –"

And I hang up over him saying that. Not wanting to hear how he'll end that.

I can't believe what's happened to us.

I can't believe what we've become.

No good end to that sentence. Hanging up is the best of nothing but bad choices.

Click.

The phone rings again before I've even set it down. This time I don't answer with a funny line. I just say, "Liam, I told you –"

The person on the other end of the line laughs. Just a hard, sharp burst. Low voice. A man. Other than that, he doesn't say anything. Still, that laugh is enough to tell me that I'm not on the line with Liam anymore. And it's enough to raise the hairs on my arms, the back of my neck. Something about it sounds... *off*.

I wait. The laugh dies, replaced by silence.

"Hello?"

Still nothing. More quiet. And for some reason the hairs on the back of my neck aren't just standing up, they feel like they're pulling out at the roots.

This is wrong. Something's wrong.

I pull the phone away from my ear. It's either a wrong number or a perv, and either way the best way to deal with it is just to hang up and move on. Disengage.

The laugh – that low, hard snap of a laugh – belts out again as I turn the phone off. The beep of the phone turning off cuts the laugh in half, but for some reason it sounds familiar this time. Like it's the laugh of someone I know.

Someone I fear.

The car's already running when I toss my backpack in and then get in myself. "Who was it?" says Dad. He looks strange. Worried. Like maybe he was listening in, maybe he knows all about me and Liam, maybe more.

I suddenly feel like I'm looking not at my dad, but a stranger. Something that looks like him, but isn't. Something come to gain my trust and then cut me down.

No. That's stupid. That's just the dream and everything that happened and everything you're worried about.

Get a grip, Mel.

Easy for you *to say.*

"It was a wrong number," I say.

Dad doesn't move. For a second I think he's going to tell me something.

Then he puts the car in reverse and pulls out of the driveway.

I try not to think of the dream. Standing in my father's shoes as he guns a man down and is shot himself.

I try not to think of the phone call. A dark laugh that cuts off with the finality of a bullet.

I fail at both.

The ride to school is short, but it takes forever. Dad and I usually talk and joke. The last month there hasn't been much talking, and no jokes at all.

Mom died when I was five, and I know I'm damaged over that. Mommy issues galore, and woe unto any guy I end up with who looks like he's going to bail. I'll cut off his junk.

I don't take well to the idea of people leaving me.

So Dad's "bad day at work" (as he calls it) did a number on me. And yes, I know it, but knowing doesn't mean you can always fix it. Just like telling someone who's had a crap day, "Cheer up!" usually doesn't help them feel better, me knowing that my fear of losing Dad was just as much about Mom dying doesn't mean I can keep myself from freaking out.

He pulls up to the curb across from the high school. A couple of my friends walk by, but they don't stop or even say hi. Another casualty of the weirdness of the past month. Everything changed. It doesn't help that my dad is a cop, which isn't a super-popular career for the significant portion of the student body that smokes weed or gets drunk or does any of the million other things they know could get them railroaded into a holding cell.

So we sit in a sea of students, all flowing toward the school. But at the same time, it's just him and me. We are alone. And that's fine. I need to be alone with him. I can't leave him. Not yet.

He waits. Dad can be surprisingly patient when he has to be.

"You could get hurt again," I finally say. My go-to argument, but it's my best one and I'm not shy about using it.

The sea of students passing our car has slowed to a trickle. The first bell will sound soon. I'll be late.

"I won't, Melly Belly."

"You could. And I hate that you call me that. I'm not two anymore." Dad grins at my irritation. The only good things about his pet name for me are a) that he's never called me that in front of anyone – *anyone*, even Liam doesn't know about it – and b) when I turned twelve he finally dropped the original version of the nickname so it went from "Melly Belly Full of Jelly" to the more *mature* "Jelly Belly."

Dad looks at the last few kids walking by. None of them look at him. "What about Liam?" he says. "Don't you want to see your boyfriend?"

"We're on a break."

"That's too bad."

My eyes roll so hard and fast it was a miracle they don't flip right out of their sockets. "Don't pretend you didn't know. It's been pretty obvious."

"Well, I wanted to give you space. Let you work out whatever it is. I know you'll do right by him and by yourself."

Dad's known Liam almost as long as he's known me; he's almost as much a part of the family as I am.

He flicks the "master unlock" button on his door. The door locks all rise with a click. "Maybe you should talk to him." He smiles, like, "Go on, you'll do fine!"

I respond by flicking the "lock" button on my side. All the door locks drop back down into their cozy "no-one-in-no-one-out" position.

Dad just stares for a long time. No more students outside. The bell rings. Faint across the street, but audible – the final call to everyday business.

"Sometimes you remind me of your mom," Dad says.

"You only say that when I'm about to win an argument."

"That's when I like you least." He smiles and shakes his head. Puts the car in gear. "I gotta go to work." The smile disappears when he says that, and I know that no matter what I say, this is non-negotiable.

"I know," I say.

His smile returns. Just a little. "Lucky for you it's Bring-Your-Pigheaded-Idiot-Kid-to-Work Day."

We pull away from the curb.

I smile, too.

The nightmare is still there. Just like the past. Things never disappear completely, they just fade.

But for now, fading is enough. We work with what we have.

4

I'm waiting for Dad when he comes out of the locker room. He looks handsome. Dressed in his blue uniform, black boots, black belt that always makes me think of Batman with his utility belt full of gizmos and gadgets for fighting crime. It's nicer than the State Police uniform he used to wear. Dad shifted over to work as a regular beat cop with the city because he said "State Police are just glorified traffic cops" and the city police department offered "more opportunity for advancement."

That was code for, "I can maybe send you to college, Mel." So seeing him in his blues always makes me feel special. Because he really had liked working with the State Police, and he had changed uniforms solely to give me a better life.

I love my dad. Not cool to say, but true.

As he leaves the locker room, another beat cop approaches him. His name's Glenn James. I like him. We've gone to a couple barbecues at his house. His wife is gorgeous, and they have three beautiful little girls that they both adore. Sometimes I imagine what life would be like if Mrs. James was my mom. When that happens I usually go tell Dad to start dating and he tells *me* he can't because who could he possibly date who would measure up to the other woman in his life?

Dad's a cornball.

Glenn is also Jedediah Voss's partner. But Voss was riding solo the day of the shootout because Glenn was out with food poisoning. Probably some cootie he picked up at one of the disgusting roadside food stands these guys are always eating at.

Anyway, Glenn's flying solo now. Voss got shot up pretty bad that day. Dad says he can barely walk, has to get around with a pair of canes. And even if he manages to fully recover is, rumor is he's *still* not coming back. Being shot can do that to you.

I can't imagine what Glenn is feeling. How it would feel to be out on the day your partner – a guy who's a bit of a d-bag, but still the guy whose back you're supposed to have – gets perforated. It's gotta be eating at him. It'd eat at me, at least.

Glenn says, "Latham!" and Dad turns around.

"What's up, Glenn?" says Dad.

Glenn shakes his hand. "You know you don't have to come back in so soon. Cap said he'd give you all the time off you need."

Dad looks over Glenn's shoulder. His eyes find mine and he winks, as if to say, "Don't pay attention to this guy. It really wasn't a big deal."

"What else am I gonna do?" says Dad. "Sit at home?" He punches Glenn's shoulder. "I missed you guys."

"Well, if I could sit at home and get paid, I'd be all over that. But… to each his own."

Glenn walks off, shaking his head like Dad's crazy. And of course, *that's* crazy since Glenn is in the same boat:

they both lost partners. Though Dad's loss was more permanent, more complete. And he actually liked his partner, so that makes it even worse.

Still, it's typical of these guys: worry about everyone else, pretend everything's fine with themselves. Divorce rates are high among police, and sometimes I wonder if that would be different if more of them could just suck it up and admit they need help and a hug sometimes.

Glenn stops walking away. Turns. "Latham?"

"Yeah, Glenn?" says Dad.

Suddenly the air changes. The banter disappears before Glenn even says it, says what I know – and Dad knows – what he's going to say. "Sorry about Steve. He was a good man."

Then Glenn leaves. Turns on his heel and is gone, just like that. Which is the best thing he could do, I guess, after saying that.

He shouldn't have said it at all.

Steve – laughing Steve, jolly Steve, dead Steve – already had his funeral. Already heard his goodbyes. And no one – Dad least of all – needs to hear them anymore. His partner is gone, and nothing will let him forget that.

Maybe that's why he let me come tonight. So that he'd have a partner, and wouldn't have to ride around with a ghost.

Dad joins me and we walk through the hall. Heading to the briefing room. "Okay, so the rules –"

"I know. Keep my yap shut. Pretend I don't exist. Keep my yap shut."

He punches *me* in the shoulder now. Trying to pretend the conversation with Glenn didn't happen. That all is normal, all is well. It works. For some reason that punch makes me feel delicious, like I'm one of the guys. Or like he doesn't just love me, but actually *likes* me.

"You got it."

And I do. Technically no one but the current shift is supposed to be in the room for the morning briefing, just like no one is supposed to be in a patrol car but its assigned officers – along with anyone he or she is bringing in for processing. Sometimes John Q. Public gets to do a ridealong – usually curious citizens who wonder what it's "really" like to be a cop – but that comes with a bunch of paperwork and a background check. And minors don't get ridealongs. Ever.

But I am going to be in the briefing. And I am going to ride with Dad. Because cops' kids get a few perks. I am going to play hooky, and I get to watch my dad do his thin blue line thing.

Even though he's still in every bit of the danger I worried about, it makes me feel better to be there with him. Sometimes we need to be with someone, even if it isn't rational, even if being with them won't change a single thing.

When Dad and I walk into the briefing room, everyone else is already there. A few of the cops start clapping. Dad looks embarrassed.

"Okay, okay," says the guy at the desk in front of the room. He's got the same blue uniform, but stripes on the arm mark him as the sergeant in charge of this shift. His name's Sergeant Tom Ricard, but everyone just calls him Sarge.

I know him, have known him most of my life. Dad loves him. He came up with Dad and Linde, but he was always the leader. Always the one with the ideas, the ways to move forward and make things better. That's why he's Sarge. He's the guy who would die for Dad. The guy – other than Linde – that I know Dad would take a bullet for without thinking twice.

Only when he's behind the desk there's no sense of brotherhood, no sense of the love I feel during backyard barbecues and beach trips. Sarge looks almost as fun as a battery acid enema. "Sit down, Latham."

Sarge is also Liam's dad. That's how I met Liam: at a cop barbecue when we were both so young we still thought Transformers were cool. I thought Liam was neat back then. That's actually how I thought of him: "Neat." He liked the same games I did. He was good at dodgeball. He was my pal.

Then one day I realized he had stopped being "neat" and somehow became "cute." A few days later he was "gorgeous." Tall, tan. Big arms and a strong jaw that seemed older than seventeen. But when he smiled there was still that kid in there, that kid who got so excited about Transformers it was like watching Heaven all wrapped up in a little boy package. A gift.

Liam and I have been dating for three years. Everyone expects us to stay together. To get married. The proof of that is that no one jokes about it anymore; no one makes fun. It's just quietly accepted.

But now… since that moment when I realized life is so short… I've wondered whether things *should* be quietly accepted. Maybe I should move on. Maybe he should.

Or maybe not.

I don't know. I don't know anything.

Sarge ignores me, per standard protocol. Dad makes his way to his desk. I stay next to the door, trying to think small and invisible thoughts.

Sarge says, "All right, now that our conquering hero is here –"

"Sarge?" Knight, another cop who was with Dad that day – and so has a permanently recurring guest spot in my nightmares – raises his hand.

"Yeah, Knight?"

"How come no one clapped when me and Z came in?"

Sarge shakes his head and his expression makes it clear he wonders how he got stuck in the Idiot Ward of this particular precinct. "Because you and Zevahk weren't lucky enough to get wounded."

Zevahk raises his hand. "Yes, Officer Zevahk?" says Sarge. Looking like he regrets the words immediately.

"So if I shoot myself I'll get applause?"

"Only if it's fatal," one of the other cops yells out.

Everyone laughs. Even Sarge almost smiles. "All right, boys and girls, can we get to work? Or should I just let the captain know that we're all quitting for a thrilling career in standup comedy?"

Everyone quiets down – more or less. Dad winks at me. I wink back. Sarge glances in my direction. Then looks back at the assembled officers. He goes through the normal announcements, showing pictures of persons of interest on the big screen at the front of the room to the usual jokes and sarcastic comments: "Hey, she's a treat," "When'd your momma go back to jail, Lundstrom?" "Joke's on you, Rice – I know she ain't in jail 'cause I saw her stripping at the Peppermint with you last night."

And Sarge, standing there like the Big Poppa. Letting them joke just enough to have that feeling of family, but never enough to let the briefing go off the rails.

After the POI photos, Sarge brings up a video about a new way to escape from an attacker who has someone in full mount position. "I want you all practicing this escape forty minutes this week. Feldman, you can use this to get away from that fugly boyfriend of yours."

The officers watch the video with probably more interest than they did the persons of interest. I'm happy to see it's an escape I already know. Dad taught me how to throw a punch when I was six, and I've been in different styles of karate off and on since I was eight.

"Okay, a few changes to patrol zones for this shift," Sarge says after the vid. "Zevahk and Knight, you guys are rolling in fourteen."

"That's not our area," says Knight.

"Yeah," says Zevahk.

"I'll register your complaints with your mommies. You're in fourteen." Sarge looks down at some notes, then picks up a black ticket book. "And this. Do you guys know what this is?"

"You sister's list of STDs?" says another cop – a woman named Shana who looks tough enough to take on a T-rex and win two out of three. Everyone laughs.

Sarge doesn't bat an eye. "She keeps that in a *green* book, Hardin. And your name's in it. This," he says, waving the thin black book, "is a ticket book. You are all expected to use it from time to time. If you're working on something else, fine, but then I expect *paperwork*. So either you're busting someone, or you're *writing a report* about busting someone, or you're writing tickets on a traffic stop. No driving around and chatting with vendors so you'll get free food. I'm looking at you, Hodges."

More laughter. Cops are a weird kind of family. They bicker, they fight, they laugh, they drink, they do everything together. It's like watching an intense Christmas dinner every time you put more than three of them in a room.

"Okay, kids." Sarge slaps his ticket book down, a sharp noise that reminds me of the gunshots in my dream. "Last reminder: lots of R&R moving around these days. The DEA is in charge of stuff like that, we lowly uniforms just write tickets and run drunks into the tank. But still, *occasionally* we make a difference. So keep your eyes peeled." Everyone gets quiet when he says that. It's Greek to me, but it seems to be something important. The joking and laughter end. Suddenly I'm not in a big family room, I'm in a room full of people who put life and limb on the line day in and day out to make a difference.

I'm proud to be here. Even without understanding the details, I know these are good people who are trying to help a world full of people who sometimes want nothing more than to dive into the deepest kinds of darkness.

Sarge slaps down the ticket book again. Another gunshot slap. He smiles a tight, serious smile.

"Let's go to work."

5

I've seen the garage dozens of times. It still strikes me as a weird place. Don't know why. Just something about the perfect lines of black and white V8 Dodge Chargers and Ford Crown Vics. They seem so orderly, which I guess represents what these men and women are about: order. But then they start pulling out and it's like the seeds of disorder are there before they've even left the garage.

Dad nods me around to the passenger side of his car. It's a Charger with a big white "42" on the roof, just behind the LED lights. I made the mistake of looking at those things once when Dad flared 'em. Thought I would go blind. He laughed. Funny, funny.

I get in the car. Dad doesn't. I see he's talking to Knight and Zevahk.

"Thanks," says Knight. Serious, which is rare. Cops don't like to be serious with each other. It's always joking, unless they're ordering each other around like soldiers on a battlefield. But Knight... not a joke in sight. Zevahk looks the same.

"Don't mention it," says Dad.

"I mean it," says Knight.

"Yeah," adds Zevahk. "You stood up for us. You got our back, and we got yours whenever –"

"I said don't mention it!" Dad snarls the words. I nearly jump out of my seat. He sounds like he's about to take a swing at Knight or Zevahk or maybe both of them.

Zevahk's eyes flash. Now I wonder if the stubby cop is going to take a poke a *Dad*. Knight's big hand goes up to his partner's shoulder. He stops him. "Easy, guys. We're all on the same team."

He claps Dad, a hearty smack on the shoulder (his right one – and I think it's on purpose that Knight avoids the shoulder where Dad got shot). Grins so big the top of his head is likely to fall off. "All on the same team. Right, Latham?"

"Yeah," says Dad. His voice is weird.

Zevahk looks like he wants to say something. But Knight steers him away. Dad watches them until they've pulled out of the garage. Their car is a Vic, lucky number "13" on the roof and sides. It leaves the structure, and Dad gets in the car.

"What was that about?"

He shakes his head. "Buckle up, Melly Belly."

I can tell that's all the answer I'll get. Looks like I'm not the only one who took some extra baggage away that day. Maybe my being here is as good for him as it is for me.

Makes me feel good to think that. Like he needs me around. I wonder if he worries that someday I'll leave him like Mom did.

"What's R&R?" I ask

He turns the key. The Charger hums to life.

Cop cars are by far the fastest things I've ever been in. They feel almost *angry*, like they're pissed at the fact that they have to travel around the speed limit. It's only when they're opened up – when Dad has his lights on, siren blaring, the thing going one hundred-plus down Front Street – that they sound happy. Roaring not in anger but like they're laughing.

That makes me think of the guy who called that morning. Crank call?

"Buckle up," says Dad.

I do. "What's R&R?" I ask.

"What?" Dad seems surprised by the question. Like he forgot I was at the briefing, or maybe didn't think I might be paying attention.

"Sarge said there was lots of R&R moving around. I assume he didn't just mean people were taking excessive vacation time."

"Figure that out all on your own, did you, Miss Smarty Two Shoes?"

"With my very own braininess."

He snorts. "It stands for Red Rocks. It's a new kind of drug that's moving through the area."

"What kind of –"

"More than that, you don't need to know."

I think about wheedling more info from. Dad's got a look on his face that's saying, "Are you going to be like this all day? Because school's still an option." Still, I push a little more. "What does it do?"

30

He says, "Tell you what. We'll take turns. You can ask me one question at a time, interrupting my invaluable quiet time and learning things that are all kinds of inappropriate for a kid your age. And I'll ask *you* one question at a time about Liam and what's going on with you two." He pauses to let that sink in. "Or we could just let both matters drop, enjoy companionable silence, and thank God that we can't read each other's minds."

I give him a thumbs up, along with a grin so wide and winningly insincere it would make a congressperson blush.

"Thought so."

He opens his window and enters a number on a keypad. A gate opens. We leave the garage.

My ridealong has begun.

PART TWO:
TAKEN FOR A RIDE

June 30
PD Property Receipt – Evidence
Case # IA15-6-3086
Rec'd: 6/29
Investigating Unit: IA/Homicide

JOURNAL
DAY FIVE

Things get different, and strange, and scary. Maybe that's what growing up is.

Liam doesn't seem to understand. I was planning on going to prom with him. Even had a dress picked out. But now, things are so different. I know a lot of that is just that I suddenly get how soon we all die, how fragile life is.

Why go dancing when tomorrow we're going to lay down and never get up again?

I know Dad wonders why I've stopped talking to Liam. And Liam keeps calling, calling, calling calling calling calling.

Damn. I miss him. But I also don't. Life is weird, you know? Funny. Not funny like a joke, but funny like there's no such thing as a joke. But you have to laugh because if you don't laugh you'll scream and if you scream then the end comes that much sooner.

I better stop. I think I'm writing myself into a depression. I'll go outside and throw seeds at the dumb squirrel that keeps coming to our house. Maybe Dad will throw seeds, too. That would be nice.

1

"What's the first thing a good cop does?" Dad asks.

I grin at him. "Gets coffee."

"Damn straight."

We pull into an Exxon with a food mart about a mile down the road. "You gonna come in?" he says.

"Damn straight."

"Watch it, Mel."

"*You* said it."

"I'm old and my soul is already doomed. You don't get to talk that way."

He smiles to let me know he only *sort of* means it. We go in. I break right to where the candy bars are. Dad goes to the coffee. He takes it black, and usually waits until its cold enough to gag a normal human before he actually drinks it.

"Officer Latham!"

"Hey, Jan."

"Haven't seen you in forever. I was starting to think you found another coffee place."

"Never."

My dad ambles over to the lady at the counter, putting the cap on his coffee. She's short enough she barely sees over the register, but I can make out the smile on her face. Older, so it's not the "please jump me" face some women make when they see the badge. Which is good, because the few times I've seen someone look at my dad that way, it made me wish I could crawl into myself and implode.

Dad puts the coffee down. Jan rings it up. "This all?" she says.

"Nope. Everything good around here, Jan?" And here's the real reason Dad stops for coffee: he believes in relationships. Stops in to buy a coffee, chat with the store clerks, says hi to the street vendors. Dad knows what's going on in his areas, and the people know he's there for them. He's not just a "dick with a stick," which is the less-than-polite term I've heard him use for a few of the cops that believe policing is an elaborate excuse to drive fast and shoot stuff.

"All's well. Better with you back in action."

I slide a candy bar next to Dad's coffee. Jan winks at me. I smile at her. She seems nice. Seems to like Dad being around. I can't blame her.

"I like these, too," she says, pointing at the candy.

"My favorite," I say.

"I would've pegged you for..." she squints at me. "Jerky. Peppered." I laugh. I really like this gal for some reason. She's one of those souls that makes you feel like you've known her forever in about six seconds. Another minute in the store and I'll probably be asking her to go to the movies.

Dad pays for the candy and coffee.

"No Red Bull or Overshock or Zapyourheart or whatever it is you usually drink?" he says as we go to the door.

"Nah, I just end up wanting to pee for the whole shift," I say.

"So? That'll make a man out of you."

I reach for the door and try to think of a good retort. Before I can come up with one, the door opens. For a split-second I get creeped out: the door's motion was so in sync with me reaching for it that it's as though it was *refusing* to be touched by me. Like I'm not good enough to touch it.

(*Not good enough to have anything, are you Mel, not Mom not Liam and you almost lost Dad —*)

It's a ridiculous thought, but it's almost crushingly real in that instant. The feeling that I don't belong here, that I barely belong *anywhere*.

Then the door completes its short arc and of course it had nothing to do with me: just another person coming in as I went out. Two people passing through the same tiny slice of the world the way people do.

I look at the guy who opened the door, and now I don't feel like I don't belong... now I think I've gone nuts. Because I'm seeing double.

The guy holding the door open wears blue jeans, dark brown work boots. A red and black checked flannel shirt, a raggedy red goatee/wish-I-could-grow-a-beard. A trucker's cap with "I brake for boobs" written in curlicues that tamps down greasy strings of black hair.

And the guy behind him is just as classy. *Exactly* as classy, down to the exact scraggles of his wannabe beard, the straggling strays of his hair. The only way to tell them apart is that the one in front has an unlit cigarette in his mouth, the other has one that glows red at the tip.

No. That's not right... I see the red flannel shirts have pins on them. The kind you might see at a gas station or auto body shop. The one in the front's says "BOB," and the one who is more actively working on his cancer has a pin that says, "RAY."

I gawk. Then realize I'm staring and do my best to stop. It's impossible. Mostly because "BOB" is staring right back, and something about his stare gives me the creeps.

I'm a cop's kid. I know that the worst thing to do when creeped out by a creepy creep is to look like a victim. So I open my mouth to say something. Either "Thanks for holding the door" or "What are *you* looking at?" or "Some weather, huh?" The words don't matter, just the attitude behind them.

Only problem: no words are coming out of my mouth.

Bob's eyes seem to dance, like he can see the strange incapacity that's gripped me. His smile widens. "Well, hello there," he says.

Ray, behind him, starts to smile as well. "Fancy meeting you here," he says with a smile.

I'm still trying to catch my breath. Absolute *waves* of weirdness roll off these guys. Forget letting them date your daughter, you wouldn't trust them to watch your pet rock.

How I know that doesn't matter – I know it, and the knowledge has me completely mute.

This isn't like me. Once a guy followed me home after a ballgame at the middle school I went to. I thought he was weird, I got a bad vibe. I told him to stop following me. When he didn't react the way I wanted – which would have been to turn around and quietly move away – I didn't freak out or panic. I very intentionally started screaming "*FIRE!*" at the top of my lungs, then kicked him in the junk as hard as I could.

Turned out it was a guy who lived on the street – we were only a few houses away from where he lived – and he was just walking home. He was also deaf, so he didn't have a chance to figure out the best way to respond to my (to him) unheard demand before he ended up puddled on the sidewalk, hands in a tight cup around his man-dangles.

But now, simply standing in a public gas station and with my-father-the-cop for backup… confronted with Bob and Ray, I've got nothing.

Dad comes to my rescue. Which makes me feel both ashamed and grateful. I love my dad, I love that I can count on him. He's always been my hero. But I know I'm going to replay this moment for a long time, kicking myself for not being able to talk my way out of a *non*-confrontation with two extras from *Cannibal Hillbillies 7: The Hickening*.

"No cigarettes within twenty feet of the entrance, pal," says Dad.

Ray smiles. He inhales, taking one last suck on his cancer stick, then he drops it on the sidewalk and stubs it out with his boot.

"Litter laws are enforced in this state, too," says Dad.

Bob and Ray both wear the exact same grins. Grins that grow wider as Ray bends down to pick up the still-smoldering stub of his cigarette. He looks around for a trashcan, doesn't see one, so shoves it in the breast pocket of his flannel shirt, right below "RAY."

Bob waggles his eyebrows, and his eyes never leave me even though he speaks to Dad. "Feeling conscientious today, are we, officer?"

As weird as the moment was, the two guys who look like each other, the grins, the ratty beards, the looks that make me feel vaguely dirty... now it's weirder. Guys like this shouldn't use words like "conscientious." They should say things like "yup" and "git-er-done."

"I'm always conscientious, Bob," says Dad. "Best you remember that."

"Of course, officer," says Ray. Bob already has one of the double doors open, so he now pulls open the second one. He bows, beckoning us through with a wave elegant enough to belong in the court of a king. "Please accept our heartfelt apologies. There will be no more lawbreaking of any kind tonight, and I trust this is the last you will see of us."

"Indeed," says Bob, and he bows as well.

The word "weird" does not begin to cover this moment.

Dad looks like he wants to bust them. Like he's trying to figure out a way to frisk them or look in their vehicles. Police can do that with surprisingly little concrete reason – "probable cause" is a wide net that helps them find a lot of things that want to stay hidden. But I can see my dad writing up the report in his head. "Found two joints after determined the perpetrators were acting extremely polite and had an unusually well-developed vocabulary."

Yeah, right.

Dad moves through the doorway. I follow him. We don't look back. A lesson I learned from Dad a long time ago: looking back implies you're worried. "You don't look back after slapping a mosquito, right?" he'd told me. "So don't look back when you walk away from a scumbag. Not unless there's a chance he'll hurt you. Then you don't walk away at all. You either put him down or you run, but you don't walk away."

No one gets hurt here. We walk to Dad's cruiser, and behind us there's an electronic tone as Bob and Ray enter the store.

We get in the car. Dad's looking at the mirrored windows of the food mart as though he's waiting for someone to start shooting.

Nothing happens.

Still looking, he says, "So were you worried about something, or were they just so totes cute-cute that you forgot how to talk?"

He grins. Still doesn't look away from the front windows, but his grin is for me. My cheeks burn.

Before I can issue a crushing retort, Dad's radio squawks. "Twenty fifty-five."

He answers: "Twenty fifty-five, check."

The dispatcher tells him of a possible drunk driver a mile away.

We buckle up. Pull out of the Exxon.

As we do I look back. And could swear I see Bob – or Ray – looking out at us.

2

Here's the thing about ridealongs: they're mostly boring.

A cop's life isn't full of gunfights and high-speed chases. Mostly it's getting drunks off property, keeping husbands and wives from each other's throats, and lots of traffic stops.

Within a few miles I can feel myself fading. Maybe I should have gotten a Red Bull or something at the Exxon.

Doesn't help that I haven't slept a wink since what happened to Dad.

A cop died. A kid.

An innocent bystander and one of the people who was supposed to protect and serve.

And that's not the scariest part. The scariest part isn't even that my Dad was there, that he could have died, too.

No, the scariest thing is that he hasn't told me everything. He's held back details, which he never did before. And if what he told me was bad enough to send me into a living nightmare... how much worse could the rest of it have been?

"You can sleep if you want."

Dad's voice jolts me out of a slide into that black pit that I've been living in. "What?"

"Just sleep," he says. "No one'll get you here. Nightmares can't chase a moving cop car." He grins, a thin little smile that doesn't make it to the ends of his lips. No smile at all in his eyes. "I'll watch out for you," he adds. And for some reason I think he's saying this as much for himself as for me. Like he wants to believe it's possible to protect me. Like he wants this to be the one place – the *last* place – the world will ever get to us.

It's a lie.

But I'm tired. And before he finishes talking I'm already sliding into sleep. Lulled by the muted roar of the car, the whirr of tires passing over asphalt, the occasional low speech of the dispatcher on Dad's radio.

I'm out. Dreaming dreams of blood, of death, of bodies in the road, a man screaming he's coming for the cops. I hear bits of reality, too. The car slowing, Dad's voice saying the typical cop-stop line: "You know what you did?"

Then more driving. Driving forever.

I wake up and evening is pushing dark fingers into the car. This is the longest I've slept, even though I feel little more rested than I did before. I've been busy in my dreams, and my body feels sore.

"There you are," says Dad. "I missed you."

"I take it there were no high adventure dispatches."

He barks a quick laugh. Most of the laughs I've heard from him recently are like that. Not really happy laughs, but almost angry. Like he's laughing so he won't scream, so he won't start shrieking. The laugh scares me.

He's about to speak when the radio chirps.

"Twenty fifty-five."

Dad picks up the radio. "Twenty fifty-five, check."

"At 342 Canal, a 415, possible 417."

Dad pauses a second. I know that means whatever happened is something bad. Not the kind of thing he wants to take his daughter along for. But not like he can ask someone else to cover because the passenger he shouldn't have is too young for it.

Them's the breaks sometimes.

"Twenty fifty-five, got it. 415, possible 417. En route."

Soon we're driving a hundred on a street marked "35 MPH" and the car sounds like it's laughing and I wonder if I should have let Dad drop me at school this morning.

The darkness seems to push into the car a little faster with each tick higher the speedometer climbs. Like we're rushing into darkness, and the darkness is eager to hold us.

Here's the scariest thing about riding shotgun with a cop: how rarely they drive with both hands on the wheel. And how often they drive with *no* hands on the wheel. There's a radio they can talk on. There's also the mobile data terminal – a computer hanging right in the center of the dash – where info on current rollouts and officer activity constantly comes up... along with the occasional off-color joke or call for after-shift beers. Cops can also input license plate numbers, names, tons of stuff in the MDT. In response they get info that may determine whether they treat you like a soccer mom or a Colombian drug lord on your traffic stop.

The thing with using the MDT, though: it means you're typing. And reading a screen. Which means beat cops often have one hand on the keyboard, one hand holding their radio or phone, one eye on the MDT, and one on the street. If you've been paying attention and counting, you know that this leaves a startling lack of hands for the wheel.

That's what knees are for.

So my dad is rolling down Chinden, one hundred miles p.h. and counting, his eyes flicking back and forth from the MDT to the road, honking occasionally when someone doesn't move aside fast enough, typing in a quick request for info, following that request with another verbal request to dispatch.

I felt like wetting myself.

We get there fast, though. The place we are headed is three miles away, and it takes about two minutes to get there. Maybe less.

When we get there, he slows. You rush to a scene, you take it slow when you get there. Because rushing gets you dead.

Dad's a careful cop. A good cop.

And for some reason, I think we're going to need him to be both.

Night has fallen.

Full dark.

The hairs on my arm stand up. I can almost hear a voice in my mind.

Something's about to happen.

Something very bad.

3

Dad turns on his spotlight as he drives, flashing it in long sweeping lines that blanket a few storefronts in brightness. But as bright as the light is, it's just a single spear against an army of black. This part of town isn't the nicest. It isn't the worst, but it's nowhere I'd come without an armed escort.

I look at the window as though it might have rolled itself down in the past few minutes. Left me vulnerable to whatever's waiting out there in the dark.

The window is up. Nothing beyond. I see my own reflection, a vague outline that's barely more than a shadow.

Dad grunts. Found something.

The car slows, stops. He doesn't turn off the engine. "Stay in the car," he says.

"Not a problem," I say. I know to stay in the car, and I'm a little irritated he thinks he has to say it. I've been a cop's kid my whole life. I know not to shove my nose anywhere unwanted.

We've stopped next to an alley: a darker river in a dark ocean. Two storefronts butt up almost on top of each other, but there's a ten foot space between them. Enough to qualify as an alley, but not enough to drive the car between them.

Dad moves into the alley. Careful. Slow. Safe. He presses the radio clipped to his shirt and says something. No idea if it's "I'm here," "All's well," or "Holy crap send everyone."

He's far enough into the alley that I can barely see him in the dark. He's a shadow, almost a ghost in the nothing of the night.

For some reason, when he goes I feel scared. Not normal fear, not the fear of anyone when their dad goes into something that could be dangerous. This is beyond that. It's like I'm disappearing into the fear. Like every step he takes into that alley – every step he takes away from me – is a step *I'm* taking toward my own death. Like he's my only anchor in the night, and without him I'll just spin away into nothing.

I can barely see him now. But I can make out enough to see him bend over, then straighten so fast I expect him to launch out of his shoes. Then he bends over again.

A long moment. He's completely unmoving, and I start to wonder if something could have happened to him. Is there any weapon that could freeze a man like that? Is he hurt? Did he have a heart attack?

Then he moves. Fast. Runs back to the car. I expect him to go to his door and grab some police tape or his notes or some other supply he needs. He does none of those things.

He runs to my side. Yanks open the door. Then yanks *me* out.

"Come on," he says. "Fast."

Faster than I can breathe he's pulled me into the alley. Into darkness.

Into a nightmare.

4

When he left before I felt like my reality was slipping away. Now it slams back. Hard. So hard it hurts.

His grip on my arm. His breathing. The sour smell of his sweat, of mine.

The fear that I see across his face, in his eyes.

"What?" I say. "What's going –?"

"Quiet," he says. Not angry, but the word is almost a snarl. Not a tone he's ever used with me before.

Still pulling me. Yanking me along. Deeper into the alley, into that dark river of madness.

And now I see what's there. What he found.

It's Knight.

"Oh, God." For a second I don't know if it's him or me who said the words. A whispered prayer in that dark river, two words begging for help from someone too far away to hear. "Oh, God," the words come again. Me. It's me speaking.

Knight is laying there, still and silent in the middle of another river. This one dark as well, but it's the dark red of a life bled to nothing. His eyes stare straight up. For a second I have the insane feeling they're looking at me. Accusing me.

No. Just up. Just at the sky. Just at nothing.

Knight is dead.

I never liked him much. But not liking someone much isn't the same as wanting them dead, and seeing his body like this....

"Why...?"

I can't finish the thought.

Why did this happen?

Why would you bring me here?

Why is he staring *like that?*

Dad looks at me, then points. Knight's hand.

I look. I see. I don't believe.

But now I know why Dad dragged me from the car.

5

One of Knight's hands is outstretched. Touching the wall of the alley, a thin line of blood on the alley wall. It spells a word. Just one, hastily drawn with a final letter that trails to nothing and ends just along his cold finger.

"What.... What's that?" I say.

Dad's radio chirps. "Is she here?"

The voice is different than the dispatcher I heard before. Or any I've heard at all, ever. There are only four or five city dispatchers that I know of, and they're all women. This voice is low, scratchy. Definitely a guy. And for some reason his voice makes something uncoil in my stomach. Something so cold it burns me.

This, I realize, is my first brush with terror. Not just in a dream, but in real life. Not just in an imagined Then, but in a living Now.

"Yeah." Dad doesn't take his eyes off the body. I have to look away or I'll start screaming. Probably won't stop. The thing in my stomach turns over again. "Who are you?"

"Does it matter?"

Dad's voice, jamming its way through gritted teeth: "Yeah. It does."

"Soon," says the voice. "Soon." A long moment, a forever moment when the thing in my body bites and scorches and I try not to look at Knight and I fail.

Eyes open.

Finger dipped in blood.

And….

"Dad." I point.

Knight's other hand is closed. But not so big it can completely hide what it holds. Something pink, something I recognize. Dad gave it to me a year ago. A joke gift, but I loved it and have used it every day since then.

"I know," he says.

The Hello Kitty wallet is mine. No doubt, it even has the black corner where I set it too close to the stove once before making some Ramen soup.

"What's that doing here?" I say. My voice starts to rise, and I know I'm getting hysterical. Can't help it. The thing in my stomach coils its way up my spine. I'm shivering. Teeth chattering around my words. "What's it doing here, Dad, what're we doing here *what's going on?*"

Dad's radio chirps. The voice comes out. "We're going to play a game."

"I don't play games with strangers." Dad answers so fast it's like he was waiting for this, like he knew the words were coming and what they would be. Everything has sped up, everything is suddenly out of control.

I feel like I'm back in my dream.

"I don't care." The voice snaps out, twice as hard and fast as Dad's did. Then it grows cheerful. And it's not forced: whoever this is sounds genuinely happy. "There is evidence all around the crime scene. Not just what you see. Not just your name and your daughter's wallet. There are hair samples, there are bits of your skin under Knight's nails." He pauses, delivering a deathstroke. "The cops – the real cops, the detectives – will even find a fingerprint or two. Yours. Enough to send you *both* to jail forever. Which is fitting, don't you think?"

Dad is trembling. His hand shaking so badly he can barely activate his radio. "I don't know what…. Why are you doing this?"

Silence. So long it's unbearable. Dad reaches for me. I shrug him off. Comfort is impossible, and I don't want to be touched.

If he touches me it's real. It can't be real so don't let him touch me I won't let him touch me he can't touch me this can't be real can't be real can't BE REAL.

A faraway part of me knows I'm drowning in this moment. Could lose myself.

This is what it feels like when your life ends. When it all changes.

"If you don't already know, if you can't already see the answers," says the voice – the Voice, "you will." I can hear his smirk. His ugly joy in this moment. "You will, I promise you. But for now you should get in your car, both of you. And roll out. Because backup is coming. And if they find this with you here you'll go to jail and there's no way you'll ever see the light of day again." Another long pause, another set of perversely grinning words: "Are you in your car, kiddies? Time to roll. The game's started, whether you want to play or not. The only question isn't whether you play, but whether you'll win or lose."

Dad grabs me.

We get in the car and Dad starts it up.

We drive.

Dad's radio squawks. Laughter comes out of it. That monster in my stomach laughs in time.

The game has begun.

6

"Dad?" I say. My voice is small. "What's happening?"

"I don't know." His voice, the first thing I hear in the morning and the last thing I hear at night, sounds thin and strained. Not strong, but the voice of a ghost. I half expect him to disappear from the car.

The radio squawks. "Twenty fifty-five."

"Go, twenty fifty-five." Dad answers like it's an official call, but it's not. It's *him*. It's the Voice.

"I've left clues for you, and clues for the police. They'll be searching for you."

"Who am I searching for?"

The Voice laughs. That strange, dangerous laugh. "Me, of course."

Dad glances at me. He turns a corner so fast the right wheel bumps over the curb. My teeth bounce together.

"You *want* to be found?"

"Don't we all, Latham?"

"What do I do?"

"The evidence at the scene of Officer Knight's death is enough to send you to jail."

"Not Mel. She's a minor." Dad doesn't sound like he's making a statement. More like he's praying. Almost begging.

"You know minors can be treated as adults if they're old enough. If the crime is malicious enough." The radio turns off. I can imagine the man behind the Voice licking his lips. "We're talking about very bad things here, Latham."

"You know my name. What's yours."

"Why don't you call me Jack?"

"Is that your name?"

"Put your daughter on."

"No way."

"Put her on, or I kill someone else."

"No way, I –"

Another voice comes on the radio. Terrified. Screaming. "*Please! PLEASE DON'T DO IT PLEASE JUST LET ME GO –*"

Silence. Then, a whisper. "Put your daughter on. Please. I won't ask again."

My dad looks at me. Asking with his eyes: *Can you?*

I want to tell him, No. Of course I can't.

But that scream. Someone's life hangs on what I do.

I take the mic.

"Hell –" My voice catches. I have to swallow and try again. Dad takes another turn too fast. Honks angrily at a pedestrian who's not crossing the street quickly enough and almost becomes a hood ornament.

Part of me wonders where we are. I can't keep track of all that's going on. I'm disappearing in panic.

"Hello?" I say. "Who is this?" I feel like an idiot saying that, like Dad has just handed me the phone on a nice summer day. But it's all I can think *to* say.

"Hello, Mel," says the Voice – Jack. "So nice to speak to you."

"Why are you doing this?"

Another lame question from me, and again, I can hear that grin. Jack is expressive. If I could see this guy in front of me I doubt I'd have a better handle on what his face is doing. "If you have to ask, you're not ready for the answer. Neither of you."

"What do you want from us?"

"Ahhhhh...." Now Jack sounds like he's just tucked into Thanksgiving dinner. Contentment mixed with something like a compliment. "That's the right place to start. That's the right question. And in return I have one of my own: when you dream, what do you dream of, Mel?"

"Don't answer that," Dad whispers. "We can't let this guy into our heads."

A new chill grabs me, grips me and won't let go. "Was it you? Was it you that called this morning?"

Silence. Then, "What do you dream of, Mel? You dream of the day your father saved his friends, don't you? The day he almost died. The day someone almost *took* you away from each other."

"Yes." The word comes out before I can stop it. I know I shouldn't get in a mind game with Jack.

But then, you're already in one. The only question is what move you'll make. Even silence plays a part, so maybe this is the right way to go.

"Yes," I say again, and force myself to sound stronger than I feel. "Yes, I dream of that. So what?"

"So that's how this game starts."

"What do you mean?"

"You're on Fifth and Center," says Jack. I look at the cross street we're passing. He's right. A quick look to my dad shows he's as startled as I am.

Who is this guy?

"I know you don't know this, since we're on channel thirteen," he says. And for the first time I notice that we're not on the normal dispatch channel – there's been no competing chatter, just us and Jack and dead air. Dad must have switched in the alley. Must have been *told* to switch. "But I've been monitoring the other channels," Jack continues. "Your brothers in blue have found the recently departed Knight, Officer Latham. They haven't put you at the scene. Yet. But they will." A moment, like he's thinking. But I know he's not. He's got this planned. Everything is happening just like he wants. "Passing Seventh and Center now."

Another glance, another confirmation. This guy is tracking us. He knows where we are just as perfectly as if he's in the car with us.

"You're about five minutes from your first real move," says Jack. "I'll give you an extra minute to figure out where you should go. That's six minutes, total. In six minutes you'll be there. Or in six minutes and one second I call the others, the ones at the scene, and explain to them what you did. And they come for both of you. And they'll find you, because I'll tell them where you are."

Dad snatches the radio back from me. "Why are you doing this, you sonofa –"

"I wouldn't waste time, Latham. Five minutes and fifty seconds."

Jack cuts off.

Dad looks at me.

If I look anything like he does, then we're both looking very scared.

7

"What are we supposed to do?" Dad says into the mic.

Dead silence is the only answer.

"Hello?" he tries again. Gets more nothing. Flings the radio down so hard it bounces off the center console. I expect it to split in two but somehow it stays in one piece. Which is good – I suspect we'll need it later.

"What do we do?" I ask. Dad doesn't seem to hear me for a second. It makes me feel like we've already lost whatever game we're supposed to be playing. "Dad!" Now my voice whips out, grabs his attention and yanks it over to me. "What do we do?"

He blinks and shakes his head like he's trying to come out of a dream. "I… We should get you out of this."

I look at his MDT computer. There's a clock in the corner. 6:14 p.m. As I watch it flips to 6:15. "No time. Someone's going to die, Dad. We've got to move."

"You don't know that. We don't know that." But he sounds like he doesn't believe himself.

Neither do I.

"We do know it. He's got a serious hate on for us, Dad."

He looks at me again, longer than is safe. I worry he's going to crash us and that'll be the end of the game. Worry washes over his face, drawing deep lines in his forehead and at the corners of his lips. "I'm sorry. Whatever this is, I'm sorry, baby."

"Forget it. Where are we going?"

"I don't –" Then he stops. He pulls a U-turn so hard that my head bounces into the side window. My world spins in opposition to the car and I feel like puking. "The shooting."

"What?"

I know what he's going to say before he says it. Like it's destiny. Or that horrible feeling of foreordination from my dreams, that that strange sense of being outside myself.

"The scene. The shootout." He glances at his MDT and I know he's checking the clock in the corner. "He said we start with your dream. And that's the shootout. It went down in the garment district." Another look at the clock. "We can get there."

I hear the words he doesn't say. The words he *can't say*, because to say them would be to make them a lie.

I hope.

8

I've been scared during some of the ridealongs – those hundred-mile-per-hour-no-hands-on-the-wheel-knees-are-in-charge rides through dark nights on the way to apprehend some dingbat kid who's been popping Mollies like they were Tic-Tacs. One time it wasn't even that we were driving fast, it was a simple matter of some guy in a poop-colored pickup who pulled out right in front of my dad's cruiser. We came so close to crashing I could see the individual cracks on his "I BRAKE FOR TACOS" bumper sticker. There were a few other close calls, too, where I could practically smell the breath of another driver we almost mowed down and/or were almost mowed down by.

This has them all beat, hands-down. The speed is there. It's night.

But the thing that makes it worst: I don't know what is waiting for us. Whoever Jack is, he is trying to tell us something, and I have a feeling that, win or lose, this game isn't going to end well. It is *his* game, and Jack is the only one who knows the rules.

I've always known what we were racing to before. This time I don't even know what we are racing *against*.

Dad hisses, whips the wheel to the left and right one-handed. The other is on the handle that operates the spotlight on his side of the car, thrashing it back and forth so that cars as far away as a quarter-mile should be able to see us coming. He uses the light like a giant finger, bouncing it off side- and rearview mirrors, poking the drivers in the eyes, pushing them to the side. Usually it worked pretty well. But tonight seems to be the exception.

Of course.

We have a time limit, a literal deadline. So every blue-haired granny, every pimply-faced new driver, every dumbass who thinks it's his God-given duty to obey the police with as much reluctance as possible… they are all out in force tonight. Dad keeps braking, steering around a car or truck only to find the other lane blocked, then whipping around into oncoming traffic.

Forget the game. We're going to die before we even get there. Before we make our first move.

Maybe that's for the best.

Scary thought. Scary, but there is truth there. We arre rushing into night, into darkness.

Into some awful pain.

The clock keeps counting forward, while *our* time counts backward. The seconds seem like they last forever, but the minutes slam by far too fast.

Three.

Two.

One.

We're not going to make it.

Dad's radio chirps. A single word, hoarse and whispered through a thousand-mile tunnel containing only fear and pain. "*No.*"

Dad's foot is already on the floorboards. He somehow coaxes the speedometer needle a bit higher.

Thirty seconds.

Twenty.

The radio again. This time it's Jack. "Tick, tock, tick, tock…." Taunting, laughter and mad smiles behind every syllable. "Tick, tock. Hickory-dickory dock and aren't we just the three blind mice, Latham?"

Dad grunts.

Ten seconds.

"*Please. No.*" And I suddenly recognize the voice. Another one that I recognize from cop barbecues, from Fourth of July get togethers with the big blue family that is the department.

From my dream.

It's Jedediah Voss. Shot during the event a month ago, worse than Dad. Still recovering, barely able to walk. And innocent. Not a cop anymore, not coming back – just a guy now, just one of the people the men and women in blue are supposed to protect.

I look at Dad. "I know," he whispers. His face is white. So white. He looks like a ghost.

Five seconds.

Three.

Dad slams the brakes.

We're here. And I honestly don't know if that's a good thing or not.

19

I recognize the place, as much from my dreams – those vivid, unescapable dreams – as from driving by it tons of times. A beat cop's daughter doesn't shop on Rodeo Drive, doesn't even shop at Nordstrom. She shops where the deals are. And that's the garment district. I've been to the garment district for cheap jeans, for homecoming dresses. I was going to get my prom dress here, until things got weird with Liam and I didn't end up going.

The storefronts here are shuttered. During the day they have a garish energy, like they're shouting at you. *"COME IN AND BUY!"* they scream. And of course you do, because you don't come to the garment district to window shop.

But now, with brown roll-down shutters covering the storefronts, graffiti scrawls across most of them, the energy is gone. Now it feels like I'm looking at a cancer patient, a slow death come to call.

Or maybe that's just what I'm worried will happen to Dad and me.

Dad punches his radio. "We're here. We're here, dammit!"

Silence. Radios don't have static anymore, but my brain fills some in. The white noise that shoves its way into my brain and makes me stupid and slow. I shake my head.

I have to keep clear. Have to help. Have to survive this night.

"Where's Voss?" he says.

Jack's voice, still smiling, still stifling laughter that is both manic and deadly serious, says, "So you've realized who the next one is."

I shiver at his wording. "*The next one.*"

I look at Dad. He holds me with a gaze that I know he means to be reassuring, but he looks too scared for it to work.

"Let him go."

"Maybe." Jack laughs out loud. "Put Mel on."

"Why?"

"Because I like her. Because she's prettier than you. Because I'm going to gut Jedediah like a fish if you don't. Pick one."

Dad looks at the radio like it's a snake.

"Dad give it to me." He shakes his head. I can see him, know he's thinking that maybe if he can keep me from talking to this guy he can keep me out of this. But that's impossible. I'm in it. We both are. I gently take the mic from his fingers.

The main part of the radio is still attached to his belt so we're connected. I'm weirdly glad of that. Like I can't be hurt as long as I'm stuck to him.

"I'm here. Please let Mr. Voss go."

Another chuckle. "I can't do that, Mel. You know that's not how this goes down. Nothing good happens without work. No pain no gain." Those words punch me.

Dad said them to me this morning. But we were in the house. I was *in my room.*

Dad and I share frightened glances, both of us saying the same things with our eyes.

How much does he know.

How does he know so much?

"Did you tell anyone what we -?" Dad begins.

"No," I say. "I haven't talked to anyone but you."

Jack says, "Now, now, no private chats. It's rude."

I gulp. Speak into the mic. "What do we do?"

"What should have been done the first time around."

"I don't...." My mouth runs dry for a second. I swallow and it feels like I have steel wool running down my throat. "I don't understand."

"Do what you do. What cops are *supposed* to do."

"I still don't –"

"LOOK FOR THE TRUTH, DAMMIT!"

Jack's voice is so loud the radio pops like the speaker is going to blow. I pull it away from my face, the sound leaves my ears ringing.

I look at Dad, terrified. What if I just killed Voss?

Jack speaks again. "I've got everything you care for, Latham. Right in the palm of my hand. And all I ask for is one thing. A little thing, really. Just this one thing and I'll go away. Just do your job. Just find out what happened."

Dad takes the mic back. His hand shakes. "It happened a month ago. How am I supposed to find anything?"

"You're a smart guy, Latham. Smarter than you're acting right now. Calm down and focus and figure it out."

"What if I can't?" Dad half-shouts into the mic. A car passes by. Slows when it sees us standing by the cruiser, like Dad's going to jump in and follow whoever it is for speeding.

The car's headlights pass over Dad's face and light his cheeks while darkening his eye sockets to black pits. I'm looking at a skull.

"What if I can't?" he shouts again. No answer.

"What now?" I say.

He starts walking into an alley between two shops.

This is where it happened. A dark slit of a street. A black river through a darker ocean.

I follow him in.

We're here. And I honestly don't know if that's a good thing or not.

PART THREE:
DARKNESS CLOSING

April 30, 2015
PD Property Receipt - Evidence
Case # IA15-4-3086
Rec'd: 4/29/15
Investigating Unit: IA/Homicide

JOURNAL
DAY TEN

Dad caught me writing in my journal. He smiled that smile he has. Sometimes I love it, sometimes it drives me beyond nutty. I'm not sure how I felt about it this time. I think he's seen me writing before. I can feel his eyes on me when I write. Maybe that's just because he was the one who told me to do it. Dunno.

Liam keeps on acting weird. He's always calling, always asking to talk to me. But I don't want to talk to him. Ever since the day Dad told me about what happened, things are just... done. He isn't in the same place I am anymore. I always thought we'd grow up and grow old together. Not anymore. I still love him, but it's a different kind of love. I feel older than him. And loving someone who's still a child is wrong.

I feel like screaming when he calls. I feel like crying. I feel a hundred billion things, but none of them are what it was before.

So I hang up and that's that.

1

The alley is just wide enough to let a truck drive in. Dumpsters are on either side, smelling like nothing or like rotten food depending on what kind of business they sit behind. They look like bugs in the night, huge insects that might swallow me as I pass.

Dad picks up some broken bits of board. I ask him what they're for.

"Marking places."

I get it. He's going to recreate the scene.

He drops a board. This is where the man with the automatic rifle died.

Another one. This is the kid. The innocent collateral damage. Weaponless, just in the wrong place at the wrong time.

Dad keeps walking.

Drops another piece of wood. It falls in a puddle of water – I hope it's water – with a wet sound. "This is where we dropped the other guy." He keeps going. "And this is where his car was." A last board, almost at the opposite end of the street.

"Where were you?" I say. Even though I know. I know from Dad, and I know from my dreams.

"Over there," he says. Points back to the mouth of the alley. "Me and...." He swallows. "Me and Linde were parked nose-to-nose with Knight and Zevahk's car." He

74

looks that way for a long time. I know he's reviewing the event. Reliving it. Blaming himself all over again. Not just for his partner's death, but for the kid's, even for the two men who opened fire in the first place.

"What do we look for?" I say. As much to snap him out of his self-abuse as to start whatever it is we're supposed to do.

"I don't know." He looks around, his eyes faraway, dreamlike. "It's been a month, and the forensics guys already went through this as part of the internal investigation."

Any time there's an officer-involved shooting, the cops who pulled triggers get put on leave until they're cleared; until other cops and a review board decide they did it righteously. My dad was cleared, along with all the others. Linde got a posthumous medal. They put it on his casket.

All righteous kills. All good cops.

I turn around in a slow circle. What I'm looking for is a mystery. What I'm doing here is a bigger one.

Why me?

What did I do to deserve this?

I'm my father's daughter.

Simple as that.

"Tell me about it," I say. Still spinning, and as I turn the world becomes clearer. Like I'm syncing up with a merry-go-round, making it easier to see the horses and dragons as they turn with me.

"We were down there," says Dad. "Two shooters down here." He points at the board marking the car. "Both with full-auto AKs. They had a hostage."

"What then?"

"We engaged them, tried to talk them down."

"And?"

"The hostage ran." He gulps, a loud swallow. "They shot... they shot...." He stops. Draws a shaky breath. "The perps shot the hostage in the back. I saw...." He passes a hand over his eyes, like he's trying to wipe the memory away. Then he straightens and his eyes are hard. No sadness, no remorse. He's just a recording machine now, playback engaged. "We opened fire. One of the perps had run after the hostage. We shot him in the opening engagement. The other was behind a dumpster. He shot Linde. Headshot, dead instantly." He says it with zero emotion. Like it's a phone number, a line item on a grocery list. "We returned fire. The second perp stuck his head out from behind the dumpster."

He returns to the present. Some emotion comes back to his face. "I hit him. I saw his head explode."

A shudder wracks my body. It shakes something loose. "Okay," I say. "Let's look."

"For what?" Dad says. Then shakes his head. His whole body, actually, like his head isn't enough to deny what he knows has to happen. "No. No way. You can't... what are you going to... this isn't happening...."

"Dad, I'm in this. What am I going to do, stand here?"

I start walking farther into the alley. "We're here. Let's look."

"It's what he wants us to do."

That's true. But it's also all we *can* do.

Dad retraces his steps. Walking back to the car at the mouth of the alley, kicking bits of trash and broken pallets out of the way. He's muttering under his breath.

I walk to where the bad guys were. Looking down at the spot he marked where the first one died after running for the hostage.

It's just blacktop. Unmarked asphalt, not even a single drop of blood left. A month gone by and the city has already eaten everything that remained.

How can we do this?

I move on. I ignore the spot where the hostage died. I'm not ready to look at that. Not yet. Maybe not ever. It's one thing to think about bad guys dying, or about cops. Bad guys do things that bring them into death's house all the time. And cops... I hate to think of them dying. Hate to think of that possibility. But the possibility is there. It's part of the job, part of the *promise* of what they do. They protect, they serve. And if that service includes sacrifice, then that's part of the job description.

But a random person? A passerby with nothing to do with any of it? That's not just wrong, it's... perverse. It's something that shouldn't be.

I realize I've stopped moving. Standing in front of the dumpster where the second shooter died. Or maybe it's another dumpster – maybe it got carted away for evidence and replaced by a new one.

Why would it get replaced? Why would they need it for evidence?

My brain starts pinging. Something scratching at it, a splinter working its way into the recesses of my mind.

"Dad!" I call.

I barely finish the word before he's there. Concern bordering on panic scrawls lines across his forehead; draws his lips tight. "What is it?" he nearly shouts.

"I don't know." It sounds ridiculous. More so when I add, "But something."

He exhales, a huge sigh that sounds like he's been holding his breath for a year. "Baby, don't scare me like –"

Then he cuts off. Leans forward. "What?" I say.

He doesn't answer. He touches the dumpster. The thing is a big box, solid iron or maybe steel. It's painted green, the paint flaking off and showing gray in ugly patches so it all looks like a boxy bunch of leprosy.

Dad runs his fingers over a spot on the outside wall of the dumpster. I can't see what he's doing at first, then I do. Another second to realize what it is I'm looking at.

A round spot.

A round *hole*.

A *bullet* hole.

The thing looks like it creased the wall of the dumpster going in, like it entered at a steep angle, punched through the trash bin and then... where?

"Is that from the fight?" I ask. Which is a dumb question. Because what else could it be from?

But Dad surprises me. He doesn't tell me I've asked a stupid question. And he doesn't tell me I'm wrong.

He flips the lid to the dumpster back. It's thick plastic, and it takes him two tries before it stays back, leaning against the brick wall behind the dumpster. Even then it kind of hangs there, like it's going to pitch forward and clobber us at any moment.

Dad leans into the dumpster. I can hear him flinging garbage around and I wonder what he's doing.

"Huh." The grunt doesn't tell me anything, so I lean in as well.

"What?" I say. "What's going on?"

Dad points. The side wall of the dumpster – the wall closest to where the cops were. There's a dent in it. A weird bulge.

"Is that…?"

Dad nods. "Looks like that's where a bullet ended up. Went through the hole, hit inside the dumpster here, but didn't punch all the way out." He moves trash around.

"You looking for the bullet?"

"No. It would have been emptied out in a trash pickup. If it was even here after the fight ended."

I wonder what he meant by that.

"I just want to know where it went. The path," he adds. And now I understand what he's doing: he's trying to create a line-of-sight between the pockmark on the inner wall of the dumpster and the bullet hole on the other wall. I help him, piling trash up at the back of the dumpster and trying not to think of what it might be that I'm flinging around. It smells like the place that fills this trash bin must deal do something along the lines of disposing of skunks. Who died of dysentery.

Dad's satisfied.

"Why does this one matter?" I ask. "Everyone was shooting that day. There've got to be a lot of bullet holes."

"The angle for this one's wrong," he says. He takes out a pen. Looks through the hole in the side of the dumpster, then inserts the pen. He looks over the edge, trying to line up the pen with the bullet's path. About a quarter of the pen sticks into the dumpster. The other three quarters jut out at an angle so slight the pen almost lays across the steel wall.

Dad freezes, staring at the pen. Then, slowly, he runs his finger into the air. Stops at a spot that looks just like any other, hanging a foot away from the dumpster.

"What?" I ask. "What is it?"

"This is where the second guy's head was," he says.

I don't understand. "I don't understand," I say. Because I'm creative like that.

Dad looks at me. His eyes are haunted. Scared. I've never seen him like this, and it terrifies me. "It means we didn't shoot the guy. *I* didn't shoot the guy. Someone shot him from behind."

He looks at the pen for another long moment.

"It means that someone else was there."

2

I know what has to be done next. So I move quickly, up and over. In the dumpster before I can think about *Eau de Poop* or whatever delightful odor I'm swimming in.

"What are you doing?" Dad says.

I poke Dad's pen, knocking it out of the bullet hole. Then I put my eye to the hole. The wall of the dumpster is thick enough that the hole creates a tunnel of sorts. Only one way to look through it and see anything, and that's by laying my cheek against the inside of the dumpster.

It's sticky. I try my best not to gag. And fail miserably.

"Hon, what are you doing?" Dad sounds worried, like maybe I stepped off the deep end.

Haven't you noticed, Dad? We're already in *the deep end.* It *came for* us.

"I'm looking where the bullet came from."

The bullet hole angles up slightly, and as I look through it I can only see a line of red, then black above it. That doesn't make any sense. I press my face harder against the sticky gunk inside the dumpster, but no matter how hard I press, a red line with black above is all I see.

I stand up. My cheek separates with the sound of suction letting grudgingly loose.

And once I stand, I see. Once I see, I understand.

I trace the angle of the bullet in the air, moving my finger away from the outer wall of the dumpster until it hangs in midair a few inches away. "That where his head was?"

Dad looks. "I... think so."

"So he got hit from behind, the bullet kept going, hit the dumpster here..." I finger the hole, then continue, "... and ended up in the dumpster. Where it either got dumped out with the trash, or just taken out later by the killer."

"Where'd it come from? Who did it?"

Dad is white. I'm worried he might fall over. Might faint or even just die right there. He looks like his world just took a big step to the right and left him floating in empty space.

I point. Beyond the line where my dad said the criminals' car was is a street. And across that street is a line of businesses. Like the businesses on the street behind us, these shops are closed, shuttered tightly against elements and theft.

All but one.

A bar, sandwiched between two anonymous grey buildings with their graffiti-sprayed shutters. A neon sign says, "BAR," which gets straight to the point but isn't terribly creative.

The top line of the "R" is the red line I saw inside the dumpster. Above it is the darkness of the sky, stretching off into infinity.

"I can see that sign from the dumpster, looking through the bullet hole," I say. "Could the shot have come from the roof of that bar?"

Dad looks. I can practically hear him thinking:

Is this what we were supposed to find?

What are we supposed to do now?

Can I keep Mel away from it?

I jump out of the dumpster. Start walking toward the end of the alley. The street beyond. The bar. Because he can't keep me away from this, and he needs to know that. I'm in it, and the only way out of it won't be to hide, it'll be to move ahead of the game. To figure it out and win.

"Mel, wait!" I hear Dad yell.

Then the radio sounds. Breaking the long silence, and I hadn't realized how nice it was not to hear Jack's voice until he started talking again.

"She's on the right track, Latham. Let her go."

I stop in my tracks. Dad almost runs into me. I feel his arms go around me, steadying himself as he comes to a too-sudden stop. "Mel –" he gripes.

I ignore him. I'm spinning. Looking at the mouth of the alley, where our car is. Looking at the other end, where I was headed. Then up at the roofs of the buildings around us.

"Where is he?" I say. "H knows where we are. He can *see us.*"

Dad's hands, still brushing against my arms even though I'm spinning, clamp down so hard I think I'll bruise. I can feel him looking now, too. Neck craning, eyes scanning.

And neither of us see anything.

The radio turns on. "You're moving in the right direction, Latham. Keep following Mel. Keep moving. Maybe you'll get through this."

Dad hits his mic. "What are you –?"

"We've been through this, Latham. Let's not repeat ourselves. Move forward, not back, eh?" Jack laughs. It's a jaunty laugh, like a kid looking forward to his turn on the merry-go-round. I hate it.

"Keep going, Mel," says the voice on the mic.

I take one step. Then another.

What choice do I have?

3

The bar smells like sweat and spilled beer, twin scents held aloft by an undercurrent of old puke. It's worse than the dumpster was.

The garment district isn't in the nicest part of town, and this isn't the nicest kind of bar. It's the kind of place I figure people come to drink hard, cheap booze and go home to hard, cheap mattresses before starting their hard, cheap jobs the next day. Rinse, lather, repeat, and the cycle continues.

What a life.

Dad enters first, walking past a brawny guy who looks like a Sequoia with a mouth cut in the side. The guy – likely the bouncer – is sitting on a stool, and he stands when we enter.

"Wow," I whisper as we move further into the bar. "Wonder how many times his mom dropped him as a baby."

"Quiet," says Dad. "Keep your mouth shut and stay close."

Normally I'd probably argue the point, but truth be told I don't much want to talk in here. The place makes me feel dirty. I can't imagine coming here for "fun."

Dad moves to the bar. The bartender is filling up a glass at the other end of the bar, but he moves over to Dad a second later. He's as dingy and nasty-looking as the rest of the place. Short, so short I can clearly see the few greasy hairs he has left, hanging to his scalp like survivors to a capsized boat. His eyes are beady and seem to pop out, giving his face the appearance of a frog that's been stepped on a bit too long. His lips don't even seem to match, with the lower lip being about three shades darker than the upper. And cap it all off with the fact that every single pore seems to be a permanent blackhead.

Yeah, this guy's a catch.

"Can I help you, Officer?" says the bartender. His voice is as grotesque as his appearance. It makes me think of rancid oil: slippery and slick and something bad under it all. "Something to drink? Maybe something for your partner?" He smirks when he says that last.

Dad's face tightens, and I wonder if Froggy knows how close he is to getting his face squashed a little more.

Yeah. He must. Because as the storm clouds gather on Dad's face, the bartender grins. I'm sure he means it as a nice, reassuring, "Hey let's not get tense we're all pals here" kinda grin. But with the weird lips it just makes him look like a manic clown.

"Easy, Officer," Froggy says. "I'm a business man, doing business, and my business is your pleasure." He leans in close to Dad. "So what kind of pleasure do you need today?"

Dad looks like he's trying not to vomit on the guy's threadbare head. "I'd like to go up on the roof," he finally manages.

Froggy looks surprised. Then disappointed. "Really?" His mouth does this strange dance of shock, a clash of expressions I can't quite define.

I suddenly wonder if there are dirty cops in this area.

The great – the *super-great* – majority of police officers are good men, good women. They're out there busting ass to keep people safe. They make mistakes, they're human. But they're doing their best.

Still, the brotherhood is a big group. A big family. And in any family of large size there's bound to be a black sheep or two. An officer who's willing to look the other way for the right price. A cop who shakes down a mom-and-pop store in a bad part of town, or else "response times" might be too long.

It's crappy and it gives the 99.9% of good cops aneurisms. But it's life.

So maybe Froggy's expecting a shakedown. Maybe he's expecting a payoff. Whatever it is, "I'd like to go up on the roof" clearly isn't it.

The expressions finally melt off the bartender's face. All that's left are the grotesque features he is permanently cursed with. "Sure, officer," he says. His tongue creeps along his mismatched lips. "Anything you say."

The way he says it….

Something's wrong. We're missing something.

Froggy sidesteps a few feet and flips up part of the bar, allowing us to pass behind. There's a door back here and we follow him into a small room. The place is crowded with kegs of beer, bottles of booze. It smells dank and moldy. I doubt this place would get rated very highly if the city health inspectors were to come by.

They probably wouldn't dare. Afraid they'd get shot.

Maybe that's what Froggy thought this visit was about.

He opens another door at the back of the storeroom, this one so narrow that I don't know how the squat barkeep could ever get through. The door squeaks on unoiled hinges. The sound hurts my ears, sets my teeth vibrating in my jaw. It sounds like a warning.

The space beyond the door is dark. I can see a single tread, the first stair leading up. Beyond that, though... nothing. Just a solid wall of darkness leading nowhere.

"It's up there," says Froggy. "I'd go with you, but my patrons aren't the most...." He licks his lips again. "Trustworthy. I don't think I should leave them alone with the products."

That's the answer. He's not selling booze, he's selling products. Where the drugs are hidden, I have no idea, but he's a pusher. He expected Dad to ask for the weekly percentage.

Dad looks at the bartender like he's something creepy-crawly out of a B-horror movie. And something about the look pushes Froggy out of the storeroom, into the bar.

I'm not sorry to see him go.

Dad looks at me. "Ladies first?" he says.

"That's sexist," I answer. It's supposed to be a joke, but my voice cracks to pieces in the middle.

Dad puts his right hand on his gun. Walks forward. He disappears into the black.

And I follow.

4

Up and up, one step at a time. I feel my way forward, the smells of the bar at my back, hearing the creak of my dad's belt and gear just ahead, the strangely light shuffle of his feet on the wooden stairs. Occasionally one of the treads shifts under my feet, a loud *creeeeaaakkkkk* that makes my insides twist.

Then Dad goes, "Oof!"

"What? You okay?" For some reason I leap to the worst conclusions. Someone waiting up here. A knife, stabbing into him. Blood.

The dark can play tricks on your mind.

"Fine. Found the door with my face."

I hear him fumble around, and the darkness of this little stairway splits open. The black becomes – well, a lighter shade of black, I guess. Bright enough I can barely make out the wraith-outline of Dad stepping out into the night beyond. I follow.

The stairway ends in one of those little house-type structures: just a four-by-four space that holds nothing but the top stair and a door. That's what I leave through, joining Dad on the roof.

"Where did you see?" he says.

I look around. Behind the stairs is the top line of the neon sign, the straight line that makes up the top of the "R" in "BAR" just to our left. "There," I say.

Dad and I walk over. The roof of the bar is shingled with tar paper and bits of gravel that crunches underfoot. It sounds like tiny bones grinding to dust.

Dad reaches the edge of the roof. There's no wall, just a flat dropoff, about thirty feet down to the sidewalk below. Steel pins and thick bolts hold the "BAR" sign to the side of the roof. "Here?" he says.

"Yeah."

We both look around. Not knowing what we might find. Not knowing what to look *for*. We move in opposite directions across the roof, sweeping back and forth. A hopeless task in the dark.

I keep looking at the neon sign. The back of it is solid, backed with some kind of metal sheeting, so the only light we get is an ambient red glow. The sheeting is gray and featureless, a shield between us and the alley.

What was I thinking, bringing us up here?

What do I know? I'm not Sherlock Holmes.

I start to feel stupider and stupider the longer we look, my cheeks blushing so brightly they might give the neon sign a run for its money. I brought us here, thought I was so smart. But why? What are we doing here? Wasting time, probably.

Self-doubt: the primary expertise of teenagers everywhere. In between knowing we know everything, we're pretty sure we're complete asses about everything.

Dad makes a sound. Hard to describe, but my ears prick up. Because the noise sounds like a quiet, "Eureka."

"What?"

The Ridealong

He leans over, pulling a pen from his pocket. He pokes it into something as I rush over. Holds it out as I get close.

It's a bullet casing. The shell that's ejected after shooting a lot of guns. This one is long, so I'm guessing it came from a rifle. Dad's taken me to the range lots of times, but I'm no expert in spent shells.

I am, however, an expert in my dad's face. He looks sick. Not hard to see why.

"He was shot from up here," I say.

"Yeah," he says. "We didn't kill him. Someone else did." He looks down at the shell again, a cylinder of brass that glints in the red neon light of the bar's sign. Looks like it's been dipped in blood.

I'm missing something here. Something more. Something important.

"What?" I ask.

"This goes to an M4," he says.

That doesn't mean much to me. "So?"

"So that's a popular rifle... but only with a certain kind of person. Not something your average 'banger carries around."

"Who uses it?" I ask.

"Military, mostly." He looks at me. "Which would mean whoever came up here wasn't some slob from the bar. And they could have opened up on me and Knight and Voss and Zevahk and wiped us all out."

92

I notice he leaves out the name of his partner. The one who *did* get killed. Not to mention the other 'banger and the dead kid in the alley.

"So what does that mean?" I say.

"It means that we didn't walk into a drug bust gone wrong. We walked into a hit. By a professional."

He looks at the casing again. I glance at the siding behind the neon sign. And gasp. Not so much at the siding, but what I see beyond.

I see a figure enter the alley we just left. Dark, cloaked in shadows. It kneels down in the center of the alley for a moment before standing and coming closer. The shadows draw black fingers across the person's face, then pull apart for a moment.

It's Liam.

5

Dad sees him the same moment I do. We both step forward, like we are connected to the same string, controlled by the same maniacal remote.

"What the hell...?" Dad turns to me. "What's he doing here?"

I can't speak. I just shrug, mouth open in dumb shock.

I take a step toward the still-open door to the stairwell, but Dad grabs me.

"What are you –?"

Dad cuts me off with a quick gesture. "Why's he here, Mel?" He turns to look at Liam, who is kneeling again, then standing and walking through the alley. Even at this distance I can see that Liam is moving oddly, like he is drunk. "No way it's a coincidence."

"Fine, so we're going to spy on him?" I can't believe this. "What if he's in danger?"

"If he looks like he's in danger then we go to him," Dad says. "But right now the only person I *know* is in danger is *you*. And I'm not willing to risk your safety for his. Not unless there's a damn good reason."

I quiet down. Angry, relieved. Mad that Dad isn't charging down to Liam like a white knight on a steed, but oddly happy that we can stay here. I hate that alley. Gives me the willies.

Then something changes Dad's attitude. Something unexpected – but at the same time, the moment it happens it seems like the only thing that *can* happen. I suddenly remember a line from a fairy tale Dad used to read me.

"*All this has happened before, and it will all happen again.*" A boy who never ages, who lives only to fight pirates, to bring children into a Neverland that seems perfect, but is a nightmare when you look close enough.

I'm on a string. My eyes rise at the exact moment it happens. The exact moment it *has* to happen. And that's when Liam's eyes shift from spots on the ground in the alley – spots where evil and innocent have fallen...

... to mine.

He looks up at the bar.

He sees us.

He smiles.

And I see the gun.

6

Dad and I run. Back through the darkness of the night, the darkness of the stairwell, the darkness of a bar that caters to sleaze. It's like dropping into a bizarre neighborhood of Hell. A place where the drunks and crackheads go, catered to by a short devil who looks at you with ugliness and hate.

We run. Run through the bar, back into the night, back into the alley.

To Liam.

He's standing in the middle. Halfway between the dumpster and the mouth of the alley where Dad and Knight and Zevahk and Voss cringed behind cars. Halfway between the place where evil died and the spot Dad's partner was gunned down. Light and dark in a place where blackness has crept in and now rules unchecked and unchallenged.

Liam is standing over the spot where the kid died.

He's looking at the street when we run up, his toe rubbing the ground like he's digging for something. Maybe hoping to strike down and discover the blood that soaked in there a month ago.

He looks up when we approach. He's crying.

"Stop," he says. His voice is low, but still manages to crack out like a bullwhip. It stops me dead in my tracks.

Dad, too, rigid next to me. His hand drops to his gun but he doesn't draw – thank goodness.

The gun we saw is still in Liam's hand. He holds it tight against his chest, wrapped up in his right hand, cradled like a strange baby born with death in its heart.

I don't want to hear it cry.

He looks at me. Ignores Dad, like he's not even there. "I can't believe it happened. Can't believe what's happened, what's…." His voice drifts off to nothing. A whisper swallowed by the black monster of night. He looks down again. Dad takes a half-step in his direction. "Don't." That voice, that low whip crack of a voice again. Dad freezes.

I try to find my voice. "What are you doing?" I whisper. A lame question, probably the wrong question. But it's the only question that matters. "Why… why are you here?"

Liam looks at me, and in his eyes is a pain so severe, so crippling, that my breath catches in my throat.

There was a day when we were ten. Both of us swinging on a swing set in a park near our house. Higher, higher, higher. Laughing and laughing and for a moment when we were both laughing in perfect sync… I think for that one moment I think I knew. I think I knew I would love him. That he would love me. That we were together now and were going to be together forever.

Up and down, up and down. Laughing and laughing.

All this has happened before, and it will all happen again.

Up and down.

Then he jumped.

Maybe it was because he was so close to flying in that instant. Maybe he just wanted to go that final inch, to reach up and touch the sun the way we pretended to do at the top of each forward glide. Maybe he was just having fun.

Maybe he was showing off for me.

Whatever it was… he flew.

So high, so far, so long. Too long.

There was a concrete curb around the edges of the sandpit where the swings sat. Far enough that they were safe. Safe from everyone but a little flying boy.

He slammed into the curb with his right knee, and the flight ended and the screams shattered the perfectness of it all and we weren't flying lovers, just a little boy and a little girl who were scared and in pain until Dad swept him into his big arms and carried him away to the hospital.

That was the only time I ever saw Liam cry. I thought it would break my heart. I cried for days at the memory, the merest thought of the look on his face. Told Dad about the moment, about the love, the pride, the terror. He held me and told me it would be all right, that Liam was fine. But all I saw was Liam's eyes, all I heard were his screams.

All that was nothing to his face now. The terror, the pain. Everything bad and wrong about the world was running through his eyes, making his beautiful mouth into something ugly, something beyond agony.

"Liam," I say. "What happened?"

"*YOU KNOW!*" he screams. It's so loud, so unexpected, that I nearly scream myself. I don't fall back from him, but only because the sound of his voice scares me so bad my muscles lock up completely. "You know," he says again. This time a whisper. And for some reason the whisper is worse.

He looks down, rubs that spot on the ground again. Looks up again. Tears streaming. Dropping off his chin. Disappearing into jeweled nothings in the night.

When he speaks again, sobs choke his words. "I can't live without.... Mel, please talk to me."

"I will, Liam. I will. Just –"

The shot cuts me off. A single blasting boom that is louder than I could have imagined. I've fired plenty of rounds, but always on the range. Always with ear protection. Never so loud, never so real.

I flinch. Dad shouts. Falls back.

Neither of us were in danger. The bullet wasn't for us.

The bullet was for Liam.

Whenever people shoot themselves in the movies, they always put the gun against their chins. Maybe sideways against their temple.

I'd never seen – in movies or life – someone turn a gun against his chest and pull the trigger. That's what Liam did. Turned it in and pulled the trigger with his thumb.

Then he falls.

It isn't elegant or violent – beyond the first explosion of the shot. Not even particularly dramatic. He doesn't jerk, doesn't fly backward with the force of the bullet. Just *bang* and he flops to the ground like God cut whatever strings held him up.

Dad runs to him. Has his hands on his chest in an instant, applying pressure. But I see almost no blood to apply pressure *to*. And I know what that means without being told.

One bullet. Right in the heart. And the heart stopped pumping that second.

I drop beside Liam. Lean in. Look in his eyes.

The light, that lovely light in those lovely eyes, is almost gone.

The breath sighs out of his lips, pluming in the night. And with it, words that make no sense. Or perhaps they do, but only to someone who is seeing a place beyond this world. Beyond pain and fear and life.

A small hint of a smile curls Liam's lips. "You told me to come," he says. "Is this what you wanted?" Then the lips slacken.

He's gone.

7

Dad lets his hand drift away from Liam's chest. He wipes the same hand across his brow, and a thin streak of blood draws a line of worry and fear across his forehead.

I can't look away from Liam's face. So loose. Whatever was him is gone.

I hope that wherever he is, he is finally flying.

Dad starts patting the body –

(*that's right girl it's not a boy not the boy you loved just a body just a thing nothing to worry about yeah you keep telling yourself that you keep lying and maybe it'll be true*)

– up and down, legs and arms. Then he turns it over and feels the back, buttocks. He's frisking it.

I can't believe my eyes. Can't believe he's doing that.

"Dad, what are you –?"

He grunts. Doesn't answer.

"You can't do that."

"I can. I will. I am."

I put a hand on his wrist. My hand only goes halfway around. He's big and strong and in this moment he's a scary stranger.

"Why are you doing this?"

Now it's my turn to cry. My own tears march down my face, gather on my chin, fall to nothing.

Dad pulls his arm away. "All this, Mel. All that's happening. And then Liam shows up here.... It's not a coincidence."

I gape at him. "Of course it is. It has to be –"

"No. No coincidences. Not tonight. Besides, he's...." His voice falls away.

"He's what?" My hands wring. "He's *what?*"

Dad doesn't finish. He pulls out Liam's wallet. Discards the contents: driver's license with him looking happy. School ID with him looking dorky. A credit card his dad gave him last year and told him to use only in emergencies – "on pain of death, dismemberment, and grounding." A few cards I recognize as business cards to places we've gone to eat. A folded page I also recognize: the first note I wrote to him. Fifth grade, thick scrawls and loops. I told him to leave me alone at recess and to stop stealing the kickball.

The first time I found that I nearly cried. Told Dad about it, and told him I was going to marry the guy.

Dad spreads them out. To him they aren't pieces of a past filled with love and laughs and all the things that make a world worth the pain of existence.

Then my eye settles on one of the cards. I push the others out of the way.

My fingers shake so badly I can barely see the card once I pick it up. But I saw it when it was on the ground. Saw it there, and will never forget.

Twin palm trees in the corner.

A name in the corner: "Pier Point."

And in the center, written in swaying letters meant to evoke the feel of islands floating in a serene sea, a place of rest and relaxation: "Red Rocks."

I meet Dad's eyes. I can see what he's thinking: R&R, that new drug – one that I know nothing about. And here we are in a place where a drug bust turned into an assassination, with another person now dead and holding a card with the name of that new drug in his pocket.

That's when the light erupts behind us.

8

The light that blares is one I've seen a million times. But I've always been on the other side of it. Never had it glaring into my eyes like this. Never had it blasting me with the brightness of a thousand suns.

I'm almost glad. The brightness shoves away the creeping numbness that was about to overtake my body.

Liam is gone.

Liam.

Gone.

Liam.

Gone.

The words pound through me in time with my heartbeat.

The spotlight wavers slightly as the police cruiser pulls up, screeching to a halt in the side of the alley that we just came through, just across from the bar. But even though the car is moving fast – fast enough that I can smell the burnt rubber of shredding tires almost immediately after it appears – the spot never moves off our faces. The cop in the car is someone who knows what he's doing.

The sound of the car door opening. Dad turns to whoever it is. Open mouth, maybe to explain what happened, maybe to protest that we had nothing to do with Knight.

Where are the blues? The reds?

It registers that the light bar on top of the car isn't active. The siren doesn't blare. Just the spot.

Why would he –?

The answer comes in the next moment.

Boom-boom-boom.

Shots blast out from behind the spotlight. No way of telling exactly where. Dad and I are lost in the utter darkness of blinding light following close on the heels of the black alley.

I feel Dad grab my arm and yank me to the side. Behind the dumpster. The same one that failed to save a man before.

Boom-boom-boom-boom-boom....

The shots seem to keep on going forever. I hear the dumpster ping and rattle as bullets find their way to the green box. I wonder if the steel is thick enough to stop them, or if they're punching through and just missing us. I can't tell, and the lack of knowing is worse than the shooting.

The hope that we're safe, tempered by the reality that I have no idea if we are, is agony.

Dad peeks out, a quick motion. So fast I can barely follow it. Still –

Boomboomboomboom....

The gunfire erupts in a flurry even faster than the last. The metal of the dumpster seems to shiver, a death rattle that mirrors Liam's.

Hold out, Greeny.

I feel oddly like petting the thing. Whispering encouraging words to it.

There's a pause in shooting. I hear the snick of a mag falling to the ground. Another one being slammed home.

Boom-boom-boom....

The sound is relentless. All the more terrifying because it is the entirety of my world. Dad huddles with me, neither of us speaking, both of us wondering what's going on, what we did to deserve this.

His radio activates. Somehow we hear it. Jack's back, adding insult to injury. "Well, *this* started faster than I thought it would."

Dad screams into the radio. "What the hell's going on?"

"You have to figure it out for yourself, Latham. I already told you that."

Boom-boom-boom....

Jack continues. His voice finds the cracks between the rolling thunder of the gunshots. "And you better hurry. Sooner or later your friend out there is going to remember he's got an M4 in his trunk. That's the kind of thing that might get through to you." Jack laughs at some private joke.

Dad activates the radio, about to speak.

Boom-boom....

I jump in. "How are we supposed to get anywhere?"

The voice laughs. "You're bright. You'll figure it out. But I'd hurry if I were you. This guy might have a friend or two. Or he might not. But you shouldn't take chances."

Then there's a click. I look at Dad. We both know Jack's signed off and checked out for now. Pulled right out of the conflict – not that he was ever here to begin with.

I look at the far end of the alley. Dad's car, so welcoming. Not a hundred feet away, which is about ninety-nine feet too far.

Dad spins. Faces the dumpster.

Boom-boom....

He grabs the top. Begins pulling. I'm pulling with him an instant later. It's heavier than I thought it would be. Both of us have to stay down, only our fingers peeking over the top of the dumpster. The proper leverage to pull just isn't there, which means we buy each inch of movement with every muscle in our bodies. We're pulling with half our strength, muscles spent by a bad angle and the terror of the moment.

Boom-boom-boom.

Then silence.

We keep pulling.

There's a *snick.*

Silence.

Pulling.

BOOM.

The dumpster doesn't simply shudder, doesn't merely shake. It jumps in our hands, like it's ground zero of a strange earthquake.

BOOM. TING.

A hole opens up in the wall of the dumpster, passing not six inches to the left of Dad's left hand. The shooter has found his heavy weapon, the M4 Jack warned us about.

BOOM. This one doesn't punch through. The next shot does, opening a peephole directly between me and Dad.

We pull faster. I begin trying to angle the dumpster toward the center of the alley. So heavy. I feel like the moment, like –

(*Liam. His body. His blood, barely there but too much just the same.*)

– the combination of light and dark and gunfire and terror have sapped all of my strength.

I keep pulling. It's the only thing I can do.

Another shot pings its way through. Dad screams.

"Dad!" I look over and see blood streaming down his right arm.

"It's okay! Barely...." He doesn't finish the sentence. Still pulling with me. Inch by inch.

Then he grabs me. We run.

A bullet zips off the pavement behind us. Ricochet. It passes by so close the heat of it burns my neck. I wonder how much longer we can avoid getting seriously injured. Killed.

I angle for the driver's side door of Dad's cruiser. He closed it before we walked into the alley, and I wonder how we're going to get in before getting gunned down. We'll have to stop to open it. A stationary target. Sitting ducks.

At the last second I feel a push on my back. Sideways and forward. Propelling me not toward the door but the hood of the car. I stumble. Almost lose my balance. Almost fall.

Another bullet bounces off the ground. Skips along. I hear it hit the side of Dad's cruiser with a dull *thok*.

What's happening? Why is he doing this?

WHAT HAPPENED TO PROTECT AND SERVE?

My thoughts jumble. Then I tumble forward, right over the hood of the car as Dad shoves me again. He follows me over the hood, the two of us sliding in an awkward splice of arms and legs and hands and feet. Gunfire follows but can't quite find us.

Then we fall. I fall first, somersaulting right over the far edge of the hood and hitting headfirst on the pavement. I splay out full-length beyond the car just in time to break Dad's fall. He hits me hard, and I hear both our lungs explode. Breath pounds out of both of us, we both gasp and try to breathe in and neither of us can.

Then Dad manages to get to his knees. He yanks open the passenger door. Pulls me to my knees as well.

I finally breathe in. The air stinks. Garbage and smog and stale chemicals. It's wonderful. Like coming home.

BOOM. PWING.

Dad throws himself into the cruiser, yanking me along with him. He manages somehow to bend himself around the MDT between driver and passenger sides, then I chuck myself in after him and we're both seated.

This is the part where the engine won't turn over. Where the car won't start and the gunman will approach with murder in his eyes and pull the trigger on us from point-blank range as we cower in the unsafety of the cruiser.

But this isn't a movie. Thank goodness. The car rumbles to life. Dad puts it in gear. Floors it. One more roar from the gun somewhere down the alley and then we're gone.

Dad's radio crackles to life. "Good job," says Jack. I wish I could reach through the radio and punch him in the throat. "I was worried for a second there."

"Go to hell," Dad says. Doesn't hit the button on the side of his mic, so the words stay between him and me. "You okay?" he says.

I nod. "You?"

He nods. Flexes his right arm, the one that got hit. "It really just grazed me."

"You okay?" he says again.

"I told you, I'm fine. I wasn't –"

And it dawns on me. He's not asking about the bullets. He's asking about Liam.

Oh, no.

I'd literally forgotten him. Not long – it couldn't have been more than a minute or two between the time he killed himself and the time we made it to Dad's cruiser.

But I'd *forgotten*.

Grief and anguish and guilt roll over me. A tidal wave of emotion, and no way I can stand against it. My

110

arms go against my stomach, pressing hard as though they can force the pain and grief out of me.

They can't.

Nothing can.

He's gone.

Gone.

What did he mean?

("YOU KNOW!" he screams. "You know," he whispers.)

But I don't. I don't know. I don't understand.

"Who was that?" I say. The tears are back. I hate this. I'm not a crier. Not one of those weepy girls who dissolves when her boyfriend blows kisses. But this isn't a kiss. Nothing so small or so kind. "What's happening to us?"

"I don't know, baby," says Dad. "I don't know."

"What are we going to do? What are we...?" I'm bent almost double in my seat. Face turned sideways, cheek only inches from my knees. The only reason I'm not flat against my legs is that my arms are still clasped against my stomach. They're like a bar jammed into my center, awkward and painful.

I keep them there. I focus on the pain. The pain is real. It anchors me to now, reminds me that I'm alive, that I didn't die there in the alley with Liam – much as I might wish that I had.

"Pier Point," Dad says.

"Why?" I can't help but sob. The sound disgusts me.

Get it together, Mel.

I force myself up. Pull my arms away from my center. Wipe my cheeks. The sobs still want to come, but I choke them back. They turn to a bitter wad in the back of my throat.

"This is bad, Mel." Dad looks at me. "Someone's framed us. And when Liam... when that happened... I was going to call it in. Just call it in and screw the evidence at the other scene. But...." He hitches in a shuddering breath. "I told you that shell on the roof was an M4, remember?"

I nod. Proud of myself for managing that. The wad at the back of my throat has turned sour. I feel like puking. "Military," I say.

"Yeah. Also police issue. We have a lot of guys packing them in the backs of their cruisers."

"What are you saying?"

"I'm saying that was a cop car that followed us here. Police issue weaponry killed someone in cold blood during what's looking more and more like a setup. I'm saying that we can't trust anyone."

He lets that hang in the air between us, a statement pregnant with meaning. With threat.

"We have to figure this out," he says. "Because until we know what's going on we don't know who to go to for help. And the only thing we have to go on is that card in Liam's wallet."

"What does the card even mean?"

"I'd bet it's our next stop. Our next move in this sick little game. Jack wants us going to this place. He's been watching us every step of the way, Mel. He was there.

Pushing us to find the brass the shooter left when he killed the 'banger a month ago. Pushing us into place to see Liam." He pauses. "He wants us going to certain places in a certain order, Mel."

"Then shouldn't we *avoid* those places?"

Dad nods. "Probably. But we don't have much choice at the moment."

And I know he's right.

9

Dad reaches for the MDT, and as soon as he does I realize that it's flashing. Onscreen: a yellow box with bright red letters. He touches the screen and a new dialogue box appears.

"Dammit," he says.

I lean in to see what he's dammit-ing about. On a night like this it must be something pretty serious. At this point anything less than a nuclear attack is going to seem unimportant by comparison.

This is definitely a nuke. A series of numbers and letters I don't understand, but then a sentence that's easy enough to figure out: "Ofcr Latham No. 2055 Car 42 POI homcd. Dtr Melissa Latham age 17 POI homcd. Last sn w Ofcr Latham. Apprch w caution."

Officer Latham. Badge and car number. Person of interest in a homicide. Me, too.

They're looking for us.

Dad looks away from the MDT. His lips pursed. Then he pulls to the side of the road.

"What are we –?" Before I finish the sentence, I already know.

The car. Cruisers have GPS devices in them. Devices that allow officers to get around in the event they're dispatched to an unfamiliar location. Devices that allow the cars to be tracked.

We're sitting ducks.

As soon as I think that, a bright light flashes. White spears that bounce off the rear- and side-view mirrors, then back into my eyes. Not as bad as the spotlight from the alley, but nearly.

Then blue and red.

"Pull to the right and stop the car," says a voice over a PA.

Dad mutters something under his breath that would have gotten me a serious talking to if I had been the one to say it. Then I fly backward in my seat as he floors it.

He takes a corner almost instantly, and the light disappears from my eyes as we leave the cruiser behind. Then it swings back into view. My eyes fill with angry tears.

This isn't my fault!

What did I do to deserve this?

Shut up, stupid!

I feel like the candy in a piñata as Dad whips the wheel side to side, barely missing cars and taking corners way too fast. I feel the wheels on my side leave the pavement once, and I scream.

He's got his lights on now, his siren wailing. Using one hand to steer, the other flipping lights and sirens to different patterns so people hear and see better and get out of the way get out of the way *get out of the way!*

The car behind us loses ground. Then it's joined by a second cruiser and both of them surge forward like they have more strength when together.

115

And worse, I hear a sound that's familiar and chilling: *thwop-thwop-thwop*. It cuts through the banshee screech of the sirens, through the angry squeal of the tires.

A chopper.

A light that makes the previous spotlight look like a candle in a cavern brightens the area all around our car. I went up in a police chopper once and saw the SX-16 Nightsun light at work. It can shine hundreds of feet and light up something brighter than the summer sun at noon. The pilot – a cute guy named Officer Alyk – told me he'd never lost someone once he caught them with the beam.

I believed him.

My stomach sinks through the seat below me. We've been spotted from land and sky. We're going to be caught. And I have no doubt that Jack told the truth when he said there was enough evidence at the scene of Knight's murder to put both my father and me away forever.

"Dad," I say.

"I know," he says back. Two words that say a lot. *I know about the helicopter. I know we're in trouble. I know we have to get away. I* don't *know how.*

Then he spins the steering wheel. The car wraps itself around a corner and I feel the wheels on my side leave the asphalt again. My stomach lurches away from the seat cushions and tries to explode out of my throat. I gag back vomit – barfing won't help Dad right now.

The turn morphs into a power slide, and our car glances off a car parked on the opposite side of the street before managing to straighten out and move forward again. Straight into the path of an oncoming truck.

Dad whips the wheel to the side. The truck's horn blares. We scrape past so close that the mirror on my side gets clipped right off by the truck's right panel.

Then I hear another honk. The sound of glass and metal. I look back.

The two cars following us tried to reproduce our turn. Slammed into each other, then into the truck. I pray no one was going fast enough to be hurt. As if in answer, the truck door opens and I see a cowboy-type lurch out. He starts flinging hands around in obvious rage at the idiot police.

We're past the land pursuit.

But the area all around us is still lit to sun-brightness. We're still in danger. The chopper still following.

And I suddenly see where to go.

"Turn," I say.

"What?" Dad says. He looks frazzled by what just happened.

"Turn here!" I scream.

He does. And I hope I'm making the right move.

10

"Good. Good move. Good thinking, baby," Dad says an instant later. He hits the turn faster than is really safe, but it's more dangerous to go slow. The officers behind us, the ones in the chopper above – they'll all be calling for backup. All hoping to get cars ahead of us.

We can't let that happen. Not until we make our move.

Dad pushes the cruiser to its top speed as soon as he hits the freeway. Only a few miles, and if this were daytime we'd be stopped dead in traffic and the chase would be over. But it's night. Rush hour has mostly died down, and we whip in and out of cars, the usual mix of people pulling over, those who wait until we're almost sliding up their tailpipes before finally pulling over, and hopeless drivers who seem to have no clue what they're supposed to do when they see the flashing lights.

I keep looking over my shoulder. Waiting to see lights behind us. No one can stop us from ahead – at least not while we stay on the freeway. There's a concrete median, waist-high, that would keep anyone from coming the opposite direction and whipping over to take up the chase again.

But I also figure that if this goes on too long they'll just enter on an onramp ahead of us and shut the whole freeway down. No getting away then.

Dad coaxes a few more miles per hour out of the car.

I think I see blue lights behind us.

"Dad."

"Yeah. I know. I see it."

We make it to the tunnel. The light that's been following us cuts off abruptly, and as soon as it does Dad whips the wheel to the right.

I had hoped we could get to this tunnel, then turn onto an off ramp that branches directly out of the tunnel like some weird capillary from a concrete artery. The street the off ramp feeds to leads to the airport, and the police helicopter can't follow us there. Restricted airspace. We'll be safe. Or at least saf*er*.

But with the black-and-white behind us, that plan isn't as good. The chopper won't matter if we've still got a tail.

So what's Dad doing, stopping here?

He reaches below the dash and yanks the lever that pops the hood. Jumps out his side of the car and is almost flattened by a passing big rig. It honks its airhorn.

Dad flings the hood open.

Then he stands in the center of the tunnel. Right in the middle of oncoming traffic.

And the car coming his way does not stop. Doesn't even slow down.

11

For a moment I'm back in the dream. Back in my father's body, watching death come his way. Not able to do anything, to act or even to move. Just fully aware of his fear, his terror, his everything.

The car – a little red thing that looks like it's never been washed – swerves at the last second. A middle finger rams out the side window. Almost hits Dad in the side of the head.

Dad cringes, but stays in the middle of the lane.

The blue lights on the horizon are brighter. Getting closer. Can't see the car yet, but soon. At the other end of the tunnel, the spotlight of the chopper is waiting to eat us alive.

The next car that comes along – a yellow car that's probably older than me – actually stops for Dad's upraised palm. The owner leans out. "Is everything okay, officer?" It's a bearded guy with what looks like real concern on his face.

Dad doesn't bat an eye. He gestures at me. "I've got a passenger who I need to get to the hospital and my car just stopped. I need you to take us."

Beardo's eyes flick my direction. And I guess I don't look sick enough for a hospital, because he loses the concern. He leans back, away from me, away from Dad.

"Uhhh, I don't think…."

Dad doesn't let him finish the sentence. He moves around to the backseat and opens the door. Gestures me in. I move as fast as I can, not bothering to look sick since our driver doesn't believe I am anyway.

Dad pushes in after me.

"Look," he says. "I need you to take us all of a mile. Then drop us off. You do it and I leave you alone. You don't and I arrest your ass. Get me?"

Beardo nods slowly. He puts the car in gear. "Where to?"

"Next offramp."

Dad guides the guy down the road. The blue and red streaks get brighter, but don't fully catch up. Probably stopped at the cruiser, wondering where we are.

We turn off at the ramp that leads to the airport. Beardo keeps looking at me and Dad with open worry in his eyes. "It's okay," I say. He smiles like he wishes he could believe that.

"Turn here," says Dad.

A side street. Dark looking. The guy freezes. "No. I mean… please don't…."

"Just do it." Dad suddenly sounds dangerous. A stranger. I look at him. He's got a dark cast to his face, a look I've never seen. I wonder if he'll hurt Beardo if he doesn't follow directions.

Beardo looks like he's wondering the same thing. A fight erupts on his face. No telling if he wins or loses against himself, but he turns the wheel. Turns onto the sidestreet.

"Good. Pull over here."

Beardo does. "Are you going to hurt me?"

"No." That's all Dad says, and that's weird, too. I would have expected him to reassure the guy, to tell him he was never in danger. Maybe even make a joke. But all the driver gets is that single word, that one clipped syllable.

I look at Dad again. Wonder how far he's willing to go to protect himself – and me – from jail.

Himself? Who knows.

Me? I suspect he'll go as far as it takes.

The chopper is no longer circling us. I can still hear it in the distance, but I can't see it. Too many buildings and bridges and interchanges between it and us.

Dad gets out. I slide out after him. Beardo looks at us, terror on his face. His eyes rove wildly. He looks like he might stroke out in a minute.

"Get going," says Dad.

"I...."

"Go!"

Our driver burns rubber. Gone.

"What now?" Dad says, and I know he's not really speaking to me, not really looking for an answer. There might not even *be* an answer.

We're on foot. Alone. Pursued.

And now, without a doubt, wanted for murder.

Collings

12

Dad turns a dial on his radio. Listens to the chatter and turns it up so I can hear it as well.

I breathe a bit easier when I hear it – which means I go from "going to die of panic" to just "going to have a major heart attack." Sounds like the officers are still in the tunnel. The chopper looking around, the pilots frustrated that so much airspace is denied them.

That, though, is a bad sign: they know we could be in this area. And that means it's only a matter of time before this region is crawling with patrols.

I don't know the area very well. The only time I was here was when Dad and I went on a vacation to Florida. Disneyworld. And then we just took the Flyaway shuttle, driving down in a bus that drove us to the airport so we didn't have to pay outrageous parking fees in any of the garages or carparks near the –

I freeze. "Dad, wasn't the Moo Cow place near here?"

He nods. "Yeah. Yeah it was."

We begin walking. I can tell Dad wants to run, but this being the city there are still enough people awake, a few even out on the street, that a cop running along with a teen girl trailing after might look a bit strange. So… a fast walk.

Very fast. It probably still looks weird.

We get to the Moo Cow place faster than I expect. I don't know what it's called, but we saw it from the Flyaway shuttle. I remembered it as being right after we left the tunnel on the freeway, and it was an easy place to remember: a carpark with a giant cow straddling the entrance and a sign above its butt saying "Our Parking Prices Are UDDERly Ridiculous." Dad and I laughed about the Moo Cow place all the way to Disneyworld.

And Dad knows what I was thinking when I asked about it now. Knows that we're about to add to our rap sheets.

In addition to being wanted for murder, we're about to become car thieves.

The giant cow looms ahead after a few more blocks of speed walking. Sign still on its butt, and I guess it's effective advertising – I sure remembered it.

I wonder what we're going to do, but Dad just saunters onto the lot. An attendant greets us. He's got a red vest on over a dirty shirt that says "Shove it, eat it, punch it," and then the name of some band in faded letters. The tag on his vest says "Danley," which strikes me as weird.

Danley nods. "Can we help you officer?"

"Just showing a friend around my beat," says Dad. "You mind if we do a check of the lot?"

Danley doesn't bat an eye. "*Mi casa su casa,* bro," he says. Waves us in. "Just don't breathe on the Ferrari in the third row. The guy who owns it has eyes everywhere." He winks to show he doesn't give a crap if we beat said Ferrari with the expandable baton Dad's packing on his belt.

Dad winks back. Even gives him a punch on the arm. *Just havin' fun. Nothin' to see here. Definitely no persons of interest in a murder case!* Mi casa su casa, *bro!*

We walk into the carpark. Danley disappears into a little white structure that looks like nothing so much as an outhouse parked between the cow's legs.

Dad barely waits for him to disappear before turning down one of the aisles. He pulls his flashlight and starts looking into cars.

"We looking for one in particular?" I say.

"Yeah. One with keys."

I feel like hitting myself. Stupid question.

Dad walks quickly. I try to help out, but I have no light. The car interiors are too dark for me to see.

"Bingo." Dad opens a car. It's a Nissan, dark grey. The inside smells like cigarette smoke, but I don't think we can afford to be picky.

It's close to Danley's outhouse. If he comes out – even glances through the tiny window in the side – we're done.

Dad moves fast. So do I. Inside in a blink. Dad turns the key. The engine revs up. After sitting in the cruiser all day it sounds weak, just a ghost of what an engine should be.

Still, it moves the tires. Dad pulls out of the short-term parking space. Moves away from the outhouse. "How we gonna get out?" I say.

He pushes on. "Most of these places have an exit in the back."

Sure enough – two more turns and we're in front of a yellow and black striped gate. It's lowered.

"We bashing through?"

Dad shakes his head. Produces a keycard. "Where'd you get –?" I begin. Then remember: Dad punching Danley's shoulder. Not *mi casa su casa*. Rather *mi* gate card *su* gate card. Still, I'm shocked. "Where did you learn to pickpocket?"

He grins. Swipes the card over a reader. The gate lifts. "You think I've been processing criminals this long without learning anything?"

For some reason my dad's previously unknown ability to break the law makes him suddenly cooler.

We pull out of the carpark.

On our way to Pier Point.

13

I ask Dad if he knows where we're going. He does. Says Pier Point is a fish market down by the pier. He's bought shrimp and even a lobster tail or two there for some of the more important barbecues over the years – when close friends got promoted, married, things like that.

He grimaces when he says that, and I can tell what he's thinking: Pier Point is a place where cops shop. Another tie to the boys in blue. This is looking worse and worse – for us and for the department.

I wonder what this is all about, and how far it goes. That there are bad cops involved isn't in doubt. You don't open fire on a pair of people in an alley with no warning unless you intend to kill them. And that's not exactly in the department handbooks.

But is it one bad apple? Two? Is the whole tree spoiled?

We don't know. And not knowing is going to get us killed.

Dad switches the radio over to Jack's line at one point. Calls him. No answer. Jack only calls when he pleases, it seems. No help there.

"Who is he?" I ask.

"I have no idea," says Dad. "But…."

"Yeah?"

"His voice is familiar."

"Like you know him?"

Dad shakes his head. Slowly. "Not sure. Maybe. Maybe I've just heard his voice in passing. It's like…." He purses his lips, looking for words. "I think of your mother sometimes."

Those words shake me. Not just because they make almost no sense in the circumstance, but because Dad *never* talks about Mom. I catch him occasionally – usually on their anniversary – looking at a picture of her. Holding something that could only have belonged to her. But he puts it away as soon as he catches me looking. I have a few memories of her, but that's it. She's a faded ghost, a thing I recall as real, but a reality with few details.

"Jack's like her, sorta," he says.

"What do you mean?"

"Like… like I knew him once, a long time ago. But the memory's almost gone. So now he's talking again I can't quite recognize it."

I look over at Dad. His eyes are shining. We pass under streetlights, and as each one crosses the windows his eyes glisten a bit more.

"I wonder sometimes if I'd recognize your mother if she showed up. If she'd recognize me."

Then he blinks. The tears disappear, like they never were.

He points. "We're here."

14

Now that we're here, I recognize the place as well. I've been to the pier a ton of times with friends. There are some kitschy little shops, a small amusement park. I've never been to the fish market, but I've seen it off to the side of the pier – a big, swarming open-air market full of vendors hawking their wares and bickering over prices so loudly that the hum of it all can be heard from the pier.

The market backs up to a huge pile of volcanic rocks spewed up a million years ago by some eruption before being melted together into a single mass by the same explosion. The rock mass is a good fifty or sixty feet high, stretching into a steep rock face at the back, and pushing to the tideline in the front. On the top it's an irregular table, dangerous and slick at all times. But the rocks are a popular attraction for beachcombers who look for shells along the sides, and for teens who get into trouble climbing the dangerously slick rocks at all hours.

At high tide the waves spew into caves at the water line then shoot in high pressure bursts through holes at the top of the rock pile. A briny version of Old Faithful.

The market is closed now, but you can still walk through. The shops are all stalls, huge boxes now covered with boards and gates in complex systems that look both jury-rigged and ingenious, like they were designed by mad scientists with tinker toys.

Dad and I walk between the kiosks and stalls. Some have canvas awnings that flap in the sea breeze. The sound is dark, almost maniacal. The crack of ghostly whips on the backs of souls gone to forever dooms. *Snap, snap.*

The wind chills me faster than it should. I realize I'm shivering. Teeth clicking together in time with the snap of the awnings, the whip of the nylon ropes that hold them loosely to their moorings.

Liam's dead.

I'm wanted for a murder.

Liam's dead.

Someone's trying to kill us.

Liam's dead Liam's dead LIAM'S DEAD!

"Honey, you okay?"

I realize we've stopped moving. I'm holding myself, and a moment later Dad's holding me, too. Crushing me to his chest so hard I can feel the Velcro straps on the bulletproof vest he wears below his shirt.

I don't know how long we stand there. Everything disappears. The breeze, the snap-crack of awnings and rope, even the perma-stink of fish. There's just me and my dad – my daddy. My heart beats with his, and all I have is his calm to keep me safe.

I pull away. Wipe my eyes. Dry my cheeks with my sleeves.

And realize that I'm staring at something important.

"Dad," I say. "We're here." He turns to see what I'm pointing at: the stall that says "*Red rockS*" across a wooden sign hanging over its front. I wonder who made the decision to have the capitalization all screwed up. The fact that I even think about that makes me want to slap myself. Not only is it the least important thing possible under the circumstances, but it's exactly the kind of thing Dad would call out.

I'm turning into my dad. Perfect.

Will Liam love me when I start to go bald?

Silly, Liam's DEAD!

My thoughts bounce around, tumbling, each one an electrical charge that jolts me into immobility. I just stand there and watch as Dad moves around the stall, examining it. It's a large one, probably forty feet on a side. According to the words ("lObsTER, SHRimP, AhI") plastered all over the sides, this looks like one of the more high-end parts of the market. Not somewhere you go if you're hosting a basic backyard BBQ or a frat party. More the type of place that the rich folk who live in the hills above the beach send "their people" to in order to keep the fridges stocked with expensive health food.

The stall is completely shuttered: heavy plywood sheets lowered over what would be the window spaces where people could lean in and order. Dad looks around until he finds the entrance: a door that looks like it's made of the same stuff as the shutters, bolted with a pair of heavy Master locks.

Dad takes his collapsible baton off his belt. Snaps it open with a flick of his wrist. Twenty-six inches of dark metal seem to materialize in his hand.

It takes me a heartbeat to realize what he's going to do. Another to convince myself he has it in him to do it.

"Dad, stop!"

He doesn't. He swings the baton. It hits with a curious sound, half metallic *tink* and half dull *thok* as it connects with one of the Master locks, along with the door it holds shut.

The lock doesn't show any sign of the impact. He hits it again. Again. Again. Each contact seems to jar my reality. This is my dad, the good guy, the *cop*. And he's breaking into somewhere in the dead of night, after basically kidnapping a guy and then stealing someone else's car.

When did my world end? When did this new one take its place?

The lock never gives. But the lock is threaded through the eye of a hasp that holds the door shut. And after repeated pounding the frame of the door falls to splinters and there's nothing for the hasp to hold onto, so the whole mechanism – Master lock, hasp, and a bunch of tiny screws – just rattle out onto the sidewalk.

Dad repeats the process on the second lock. Then retracts his baton, clips it back to his belt, and pulls out a flashlight and moves through the now-open door to Red Rocks. I follow him.

Because what else can I do?

15

"What are we looking for?" I ask.

Dad shakes his head. "I don't know. We've been through all of it. Nothing looks important. You see anything?"

I shake my head.

The inside of the stall – big enough it almost qualifies as a full-blown store – is mostly empty. There are long troughs that stink to high heaven and which I guess get filled with ice and fish each morning, then emptied out at night. There are a few small freezers humming in one corner – mostly empty, with nothing interesting in them. A pair of cash registers bolted to tables at opposite sides of the space. Work tables with knives and other kitchen tools stowed in them, but nothing looks interesting, let alone illegal.

Dad even shined his light down each of the big drains in the center of the aisles between the ice troughs. Nothing. Just dark and fish smell. Other than the festively-painted interior – cartoonish drawings of local sights and celebrities – this is about as boring a place as any I've been in.

Dad pulls out his radio. "Jack? Jack, we're here and we haven't found anything. You want this stupid game to keep going, you gotta throw us a bone."

The radio hisses for an instant, then is silent. No one is there. Or if anyone *is* there, then he doesn't feel like talking.

Dad kicks one of the tables. It scoots a good foot across the floor, the cutlery inside rattling as it makes the leap. I cringe at the sudden noise. At the sudden violence. I don't think I've ever seen Dad lose his cool, but I can tell from his face – the tight lines of his mouth, the whiteness of his cheeks – that he's on the edge of losing it in a big way.

I look away from him.

Then look back just as he's winding up for another kick.

"Dad," I say.

He kicks the table again. Harder. One of its drawers opens and half a dozen sharp knives spill out.

"Dad!"

He spins. "What?" he shouts. Then seems to realize how close he is to a complete loss of control. He shakes himself. Closes his eyes for a long moment. When he opens them they seem focused again. Not calm, exactly, but more in control. "What, Mel?"

I point. "We're in the wrong place," I say.

The ceilings. The walls. Covered with caricatures and cartoon pictures of local landmarks. And there, sandwiched between a muscle-bound bodybuilder and a weirdly distorted view of the Chinese Theater... a large, irregular shadow. The familiar outline of volcanic rocks that this very fish market has neatly integrated into its architecture.

And over the picture: "Red Rocks."

The same name as the drug. The same name on the card.

No coincidence. There *are* no coincidences. Not tonight.

We leave the stall. I stop to close the door, which I know is ridiculous under the circumstances. But it seems wrong to leave the place open. We broke into it, and I feel like we have to close it. Even though I can't fix it, even though what we've done will probably frighten and anger the owners tomorrow.

Maybe we can explain. When all this is over, maybe we can come back.

We walk through the market. Pushing on with purpose – even more so than when we were looking for the stall in the first place. I suddenly feel like I'm walking arm in arm with fate. A sense that this is happening like this because it *has* to.

We look around the base of the rocks. Going as far as we can until the half-melted rocks disappear into a cliff face on one side, into pounding surf on the other.

Nothing. Just the smell of rotting sea life, the occasional crab that scuttles from one crack in the rock to another.

Neither of us asks what to do next. We just *know*.

We begin to climb.

PART FOUR:
INTO THE DEPTHS

```
June 30
PD Property Receipt - Evidence
Case # IA15-6-3086
Rec'd: 6/29
Investigating Unit: IA/Homicide
```

JOURNAL
DAY FIFTEEN

I never thought that something that happened to someone else would affect <u>me</u>.

I never want to leave the house. Dad still hasn't been cleared by the inquiry, so until he does he's here. And I feel like as long as I'm with him, watching him the way he sometimes watches me, I can keep him safe.

Please, God, keep him safe.

I can't lose another parent.

1

The rocks bite my hands. So rough in places, so sharp in others, that I figure I must be leaving a trail of bloody palm prints behind as I climb. I actually look down to see how much blood I'm leaving on the rocks.

Nothing. The climb is painful, but it's not killing me. Yet.

Dad climbs above me. Blazing a path. I follow him. Using his handholds, his footholds. He reaches back from time to time to help me past a tricky spot.

The mountain of rocks isn't particularly steep, but it can be dangerous. Falling down the sharp and craggy pile of rocks will mean deep cuts, definite broken bones. Maybe worse. And doing this at night is a crash course in reckless stupidity.

We have no choice.

Dad reaches down to help me up the last little bit. Then we're on top.

The holes where the geysers erupt are dry – high tide hasn't come in. Not completely, at least. But as I look, one of them whistles, a low, moaning sound like a grieving ghost has been buried below the rocks. I look at Dad, surprised.

"Tide," he says. "It pushes into the rocks, forces the air out through the holes. Some of the locals call this the Ocean's Tomb."

"Great." As if it wasn't creepy enough.

We spread out. Looking for a needle in a needle stack.

On the top, the rocks have settled into something of a plateau. More or less even, though the rocks that make up its mass are separated from one another by as much as a foot of empty space. Within that foot there is only darkness. Black crevasses of nothing that could drop down an inch, a foot, a yard. More than enough to break an ankle. To get caught.

I don't want to end up as a fixture on the Ocean's Tomb.

The foghorn wail of the rocks follows me as I pick my way forward, moving toward the front of the rocks as Dad moves toward the back. I look at my feet constantly, focusing on each footstep, trying to look at the rocks around as well but failing miserably.

There's nothing here. Just dangerous rock and the even more dangerous absence of rock.

I pick back and forth, up and down.

Nothing.

Nothing.

Nothing.

I finally go back to the center. Dad's there, looking as frustrated as I feel. It seems like we've been here for hours, like the rocks have robbed us of more time than was fair. Slowing every footstep, keeping us from our goal.

"What now?"

"We've looked everywhere," Dad says.

At that moment, the ghost screams louder than ever. A blast so loud that I pitch forward, scream.

And I know: there's one place we haven't gone.

I turn around.

Toward the dark mouth of the tomb.

2

There are three holes on top of the huge rock pile. Three major ones, that is. Two that jet water as high as fifty feet in the air, a third that fountains up to waist height. I passed all three in my crisscrossing examination of the mountaintop.

The two that jet water are small: not even big enough for a child.

The third one? Much bigger. Big enough to climb down into.

Dad follows me, and as soon as I reach the lip of the thing, he seems to know what I plan.

"No, baby. No way."

"We have to." And we do. Again I'm held fast by that strange sense of fate.

All this has happened before…

And suddenly I see that Dad knows it, too. This has to happen.

… and it will all happen again.

He holds my arm. "Let me go, at least."

I look at him. At the hole. Maybe he can fit. But maybe not. It'd be a tight squeeze, to say the least. And what if he got caught?

The tomb whistles again. Even louder. The tide is coming in. *Closing* in. Anyone caught in the shaft, in any hole below when it fully arrives will be slammed to pieces.

I start climbing down. I don't argue with him, I just move. Movement is the only answer to some arguments – words aren't enough to make a point, not enough to show *rightness*. Sometimes you can't tell a person, you have to just do the right thing and hope they get it.

I think Dad's going to stop me. He reaches out. Reaches to grab me... but he's just helping me down. Knowing this has to be done.

Before I let go of him, he hands me a small flashlight. I stick it in my mouth.

I climb down. The ghost whistle surrounds me as I descend into the tomb.

Climbing down is hard at first, but gets easier. I'm glad for a moment, until I realize that the reason it's easier is that the hole is closing in on me. The chimney that had seemed more than wide enough to hold me is suddenly a tight squeeze. Pressing against my back, my hips. I have to shove my way down a few times, kicking my feet to force myself deeper.

The sound of surf crashing suddenly rises up to meet me. With it, the smell of sea life that had been brought into whatever caves lay below, there to die and rot unknown and unmourned.

I think of the kid in my dream. Laid out in the middle of the alley. Did someone mourn the death of that one person, the passing of that one life?

And suddenly I know who Jack is.

I keep moving. Try not to think of that, try not to think of what kind of lesson we are here to learn.

The smell of rot grows, greater and greater until it gags me.

Suddenly my feet dangle. No purchase. I kick up, but lose my handholds at the same moment. I fall with a scream, expecting to tumble forever, to break my neck in the hard rock below.

Instead I only drop a few feet. Fall on my butt on sand and water. My teeth bounce painfully against the metal of the flashlight, then it bounces away with a splash.

Dad shouts down to me. "You okay?"

"Yeah, I'm fine!" I regret it instantly, as my open mouth allows more of the dank, rank smell into my body. I cover my mouth and nose with my sleeve.

I look around for the flashlight, finding it quickly since it's the only source of light down here. It had bounced into the water, but must be at least partially water resistant since it's still working. But who knows how long that will last? I have to work fast.

I look around.

I have fallen through the ceiling of a cave at the base of the Ocean's Tomb. The cave is only about four and a half feet tall, which means I can't even stand up. That's good news, since it means I can reach the hole I came through, can hopefully get out again.

The first thing I see is the water spilling in at the far end of the cave. A long, narrow slit where the surf pounds in.

When I landed, the surf was only at ankle height. Now it's at my shins. The tide's coming fast. I don't have much time.

I look around. Hoping without much hope that I might see something.

One side of the cave: empty. Not even the graffiti or beer cans you might expect in a place like this. Apparently it's too dangerous for even the most daring teens.

I swing the light around.

And my scream overpowers the ghost wail that surrounds me.

"What is it? What is it *WHAT IS IT?*"

I can hear scuffling above and know Dad is about to come down. I don't want him to. What if we get stuck down here? What if we die?

What if we rot away like the body that's wedged into the rocks in the back of the cave?

My mouth opens and closes, opens and closes. I can't find my voice, can't find air. Then I realize the water is up to my knees. Touching the body. What if Dad gets stuck, what if the body comes loose and I'm trapped down here with a corpse bumping into me until I drown?

I find my voice. "Don't come down! Don't! Just – just wait!"

Dad goes silent. I hope he's listening. I don't have a lot of time. Every time water slips out of the cave, then pours back in through that crack, it's a bit higher. A bit louder. A bit more frightening.

145

I make my way to the body. Slogging through what I imagine to be not just water, not simple surf, but the outgoing traces of a murdered soul.

Maybe it's not murder. Maybe it's just some other idiot who came down here. Some fool like you who climbed down and got caught by the tide and drowned.

Then my light shines on the body's face.

No.

Murder.

3

I worry for a moment that I've been inhaling human remains. Smelling the rot of a body long gone. But it must have been just fish, just old brine and decomposing crabs and other things that came here to die. Because this body is too new to be rotting. At least, too new to rot *much*.

I know this, because when I shine my light on the corpse's face, it is the face of a man I spoke to just a little while ago.

I breathe his name. It's a curse, a prayer, last words that should have been spoken but weren't.

"Voss."

Jedediah Voss was a big man before the shootout. But he was hit in the stomach, twice in the leg, once in the right arm. The stomach was the worst one – they took out a chunk of his intestine, his colon. Dad told me he just got out of the hospital a few days ago.

And here he is. Looking shrunken, barely a specter of himself. Curled in on his center like his wounds reappeared. Only it's not the wounds that did this to him. Easy enough to see that. Easy enough to see the way his neck is twisted around, the way his vertebrae poke at his skin.

His right eye stares at nothing. His left has a crab sitting on top of it. Picking at it. The crab doesn't flinch at the light. Too much interest in the feast.

I almost throw up. Manage not to, but I do turn away. All I can think of is that mad dash that started the night. Jack telling us we had only minutes to get to the scene of the gunfight or Voss would be killed.

I never liked Voss. He was gruff, bordered on mean. But he was part of that team. Part of the group of men who went through the Academy with Dad. Knight, Zevahk, Linde, Sarge.

Voss.

"He lied. Lied. Jack lied. He was never going to let Voss go no matter what we did." I barely realize I'm talking. The words come out on their own, like someone else is talking. I'm in a dream. None of this is real. None of it *can* be real.

But the water is up to my hips. It's real.

The crab on Voss's eye scuttles away as water splashes it. It won't take long for the salt to strip the man to bone. And with the surf pounding in through the small slit at the front of the cave, it's unlikely the corpse will go anywhere. This is a perfect place to stash a body.

My eye falls on something else. Something tethered to the side of the wall by a small length rope.

I grab the small package. Untie it from the wall with fumbling fingers.

On top is scribbled, "The truth will set you free." I grab the package. Before I can examine it further, something splashes behind me.

You wouldn't think I'd notice that. Just one more wet sound in the middle of a literal ocean of noise. But I do. I hear it clearly.

I shove the package in the waist of my pants and whip around. As I do I hear a deep chuckle.

"Fancy meeting *you* here."

At first I can't see anything behind the flashlight that blares into my eyes. Then it lowers a bit, and I see swim trunks, a muscled chest, an oxygen tank strapped to a back.

A face I recognize.

I don't know if this is Ray or Bob. And it doesn't matter. I didn't get a good feeling off either of the twins when I saw them in the Exxon station, I get an even *less* good feeling seeing one of them deep under the Ocean's Tomb, no one else for company but a package – probably drugs – and a dead man.

Ray/Bob has a knife strapped to his thigh.

"What have we here?" he says, looking past me at Voss.

"Like you don't know."

"And where are my lovely rocks?" he says. He *tsks*, then wags a finger. "Don't you know you mustn't touch other people's things?"

I stare at him, not sure what to say or what to do. Then I dart for the hole that leads away from this awful place, this tomb within a tomb.

The other man rushes me with murder in his eyes.

4

I scream. Barely registering that Dad screams at the same time, his terror washing over me, making my own fear even worse. Moving as fast as I can for the open throat that leads out of the belly of the Ocean's Tomb.

But the water is past my waist now. Climbing higher. Shoving me back as more comes into the cave, slams into me.

Then the water isn't the only thing slamming into me. Ray/Bob hits me as well. Pushes me back, back. My feet wheel over nothing as they briefly lose contact with the sand and rock I was standing on. I scream, but the scream cuts off as his hands wrap around my throat.

Now my fear redoubles. He's trying to kill me. His thumbs find the hollow of my throat. Press hard. Pain rocks me, almost drives me below the water.

I'm glad. If he knew what he was doing he would be choking me, not trying to suffocate me. Choking me would involve pinching my carotid arteries, the flow of blood to my brain. If that happened I'd have only a few seconds, maybe ten, before unconsciousness claimed me. This way, with him just cutting off my air flow, I still have a few moments longer. Maybe as long as thirty seconds. Choking, gagging, awful seconds. But it's time.

Ray/Bob is bigger than me. Heavier. Stronger. He has all the advantages.

But eyes are eyes. Doesn't matter if you weigh ninety pounds or three hundred. Some things are soft and hurt when they get attacked, no matter how big or small you are.

My right hand turns to a claw, four fingers clasped together on one side, a crooked thumb on the other. I clap it against his left temple, my thumb finding his eye and pressing. His eyelid closes automatically, but the thin wall of skin isn't much protection. Not against this.

I press. Hard as I can. Dad has drilled this move into me. "Don't do it. Don't ever do it," he said when he first taught me. "Unless you *have* to do it. Then do it like you mean it."

I do it like I mean it. Do I ever.

Now I'm not the only one screaming. And Ray/Bob's screams are louder, more panicked than mine. Pain rides along the walls and ceiling of the cave. Bounces on the top of the frothing surf that still pounds into the space around us. Suddenly his weight is off me.

I think for a beautiful instant that I have the upper hand. That the lessening of weight means he's giving up and letting me go.

Then I realize I'm nearly floating. The water is up to my chest. Ray/Bob's weight coming away is just a sign that I'm going to drown if I stay down here much longer.

His hands dropped away for a second when I gouged his eye. Now they're back, harder than ever. I feel like some kind of machine is digging into my throat. The darkness of the cave is thickening into a deeper darkness that gathers at the corners of my vision and begins to crawl in black ink streaks across my eyes.

I'm going to die here. Down in the dark, to lay forever with another dead man as my only company.

My hands scrape and scratch against Ray/Bob's hands, but he's too strong. I reach for his other eye with my left hand, but he's ready this time, and pulls his head away. I can't kick or punch him effectively, either, not with all the water sucking all the force out of my movements.

He pulls me closer. "Kill you!" he screams. Something splashes my face – spit or blood or just splashing water, I'm not sure. "I'll *kill you, bitch!*"

Closer, so he's almost hugging me. Like he wants to feel the moment I lose consciousness, the very instant the life leaves my body.

Closer. Closer.

I let him. One last chance.

Blackness everywhere. Death coming in the dark of the cave, the thick night of a forever sleep.

I grab the knife off his sheath.

He realizes it's happening, tries to pull away. The hold on my throat releases, and now bright white flashes replace the heavy darkness of only a moment below. I'm still blind, but it's a gorgeous blindness. The surreal visionless vision of life flooding back into my lungs.

I stab with the knife. Just moving on instinct. Not thinking. If I think about it, I might not do it.

The knife hits something. Something hard and soft at the same time. Thick, slow, heavy.

Ray/Bob screams.

I keep pushing.

Screaming.

Hard soft push... push... push....

Screaming.

The knife jerks out of my hand. Still embedded in flesh.

The screaming silences.

The water is up to my neck.

I'm alone.

5

I've stayed too long. Only inches between the incoming surf and the top of the cave. I'm more swimming than walking. Pulling myself back to the hole that leads out of what has become a very literal tomb. But I lost my light in the fight, as did Ray/Bob. There is only darkness around me. I don't know where I am, or where my exit – my escape – is.

The water won't let me go. It's pushing in more than flowing out. The surge slams me back, my hand goes behind me.

The hand that flies behind me falls into something soft. I gag back a scream. I thought Voss's body would be rigid. Maybe rigor hasn't had a chance to set in.

Then those thoughts are slammed out of my head by an influx of water that goes over my mouth. Seawater pounds into my nose, my throat. I inhale. Choke. Gasp. Inhale more seawater. Try to push forward and can't.

Can't...

Can't.

I jam my face against the top of the cave. One more breath.

Then I'm under. Just me and water and a pair of dead men in the dark.

6

It's almost peaceful. A part of me wants to just give up. Stay here. Let the water – the darkness – take me and own me.

No. Dad. What would he do without me?

A foolish thought. A *ridiculous* thought. But it gets me moving.

Only problem: I have no idea where I am. No idea where my exit is.

I start to panic. The slit the water is pouring through is now a high-pressure jet. It would cut me in half before I got within ten feet, let alone permitting me to leave. And I still don't know where I am in relation to the hole I came in through.

I think for a moment about finding Ray/Bob and stripping his scuba equipment off him. Using it to wait out the tide. Only problems are I have no idea where he is in here. And even if I found him, I've never used scuba gear and I'd probably drown – even assuming there was enough air in the tank to do what I wanted to in the first place.

I start to claw at the water. My lungs are burning. My body starting to panic of its own accord.

I'm going to die here.

I force my hands to slow. Force my body to stop. Reach. Turn a circle.

I bump a familiar shape. Something scuttles under my hand and I wonder if that crab has come back for seconds. Because I've got both hands on Voss now. One on his shirt, one on the rocky outcroppings of his broken neck bones.

I don't even shudder. It's the best feeling ever. Because it tells me where I am.

My hands go up. Touching the ceiling. I use it as an anchor, my feet leaving the ground completely. Pulling hand over hand, trying to –

(*ignore the feel of my lungs the pound in my head the need to breathe need to BREATHE*)

– control the urge to panic, to flail my way instead of feeling my way forward.

The waves still shove me back. I try to time my pulls with the outflows, holding fast when I feel the waves pounding in. The sound of surf is all I can hear. Then another sound intrudes.

A moan.

I think for a moment it must be me. But that's impossible: I'm still under water.

It's the Ocean's Tomb. I'm close enough to the chimney that leads to freedom that I'm hearing its whistle. I follow the sound now. And suddenly one of my reaching hands plunges *up*.

I've found the shaft. Found my exit.

And, I realize, found more water. There's no air here, just more surf, shoving its way ever higher in the empty column. It never sprays out of this hole in a jet – the hole is too wide to create that kind of pressure – but it looks like it fills it up well enough. Maybe even reaches all the way to the top and spills over the sides.

I pull myself up.

Not going to make it.

And it's true. My body's need for air is about to override my ability to keep my mouth shut. I'm going to open wide and inhale in a few seconds, and it won't matter whether I'm surrounded by oxygen or H2O. I'll suck water, then I'll convulse, then I'll die.

I wonder if that'll make Jack happy or sad. I won't learn his lesson.

Or maybe I will. Maybe death is the lesson he intends.

I keep pulling up. My body in the chimney of rock. I'm going to open my mouth.

The water sucks down below me. Pulls at me in the shaft, and I hope that the level might lower enough for me to break the surface and breathe.

No such luck.

I open my mouth.

I inhale.

7

It's not as bad as I thought it would be.

It's far worse.

The water goes down like acid, then rushes back out as I cough, gag. More water streams into my mouth. I can't help it. My hands claw upward, all semblance of control absolutely gone.

This is the worst terror I have ever known. I feel heavy, like my terror is weighing me down, dragging me under the water.

Then the sea – which surged down a moment ago – blasts upward. And I go with it. My body slams around like a pinball, banking off one wall of the shaft and then another. My hands, still clutching and grabbing up like they hope to hook the sky itself, manage to grab a small outcropping. I haul myself up, still gagging and throwing up, as the water shoves me violently from behind.

And suddenly my head is above water.

I still can't breathe for a moment. Still can't inhale, like my body has forgotten how to do that in the moments that breathing was denied it.

Then, suddenly, all I *can* do is breathe. Just clinging to the side of the shaft, pressing my sandy, salty cheek against the wet rock and sucking in so much air I feel like I might pop.

I hear screams. Dad. Shouting, shrieking. Terror clear in his voice. My name sounding over and through the darkness of the shaft.

I can't answer. I can climb, or I can speak. But I can't do both. It's not cruelty, I just don't have the strength.

And them I'm out.

I collapse in Dad's arms.

I feel like I've just been born. Or perhaps like I've just died. Maybe the two are more the same than we know. Not two sides of the same coin, but more like dawn and dusk – they look so much the same you almost can't tell which is which unless you know which way the sun is moving. Time tells the secret, but the look is much the same. Both have their roots in pain, in blood, in fear.

I look up at the moon. The thing that pulled the water close, that called it to kill me.

I wonder if I'll ever look at the moon the same again. Or the beach.

Probably not.

Dad's sobbing. "I thought I lost you. I can't lose you, baby. Not like Mom. Can't lose you like Beck. Not like Beck."

He goes on, crying. Then he's done. And now it's *my* turn to cry. I tell him what happened in the cave, long sentences cut in small pieces by shuddering cries that seem to pull my soul apart. When I get to Voss he pulls me tight. When I tell about Ray/Bob and having to gouge his eye then kill him, he doesn't move at all. Just whispers, "Oh, my baby," and stays absolutely still.

Then I'm done. All is quiet. Even the tomb stops its mournful shrieking cry for a time.

We stay like that. I don't know how long. I don't care. For that one long slice of my life all that matters is my dad, holding me. Cradling me. Knowing that he'll always be there for me just like I'll always be there for him.

Family.

Even though I've seen awful things tonight – Knight's dead body, Liam pushing a gun into his chest and pulling the trigger, Voss's corpse with its one-eyed stare, killing a man – all that suddenly matters less than this moment. Like as long as Dad holds me, nothing can touch us. We'll beat whatever this is, as long as we're together.

Something's digging into my back.

I twist. Pull it out.

The package.

"The truth will set you free," I murmur.

Dad looks at it. He laughs. But the laugh is without humor. And when he helps me stand and takes the package, there is something terrible in his eyes.

I see, for the first time, the man who can pull a gun if need be. A man who can hurt others.

A man who can kill.

8

"Dad," I say. And when I'm not sure he even hears the word, I repeat it. "Dad? You okay?"

I wish I could take back the words as soon as I say them. If stupidity could kill, I would have just leveled the city. Of *course* he's not okay. Neither of us is okay. We've been beaten up, knocked down, run around, nearly drowned.

I killed a man.

(*killed a man killed a man killed a man*

just like the men in the alley just like whoever we're hunting just like the ones who

killed a man killed a man killed a child

when will I forget when can I forget oh please let me forget)

I try to focus on Dad. He's worried for me more than for himself, I know – but that doesn't mean he's all right. Loving someone else and wanting the best for them doesn't mean you lose your own needs. It just means you push them away. Shove them deep, to deal with later or never at all.

I wonder, for a second, if that's what makes a good parent: the ability to push away self an infinite number of times.

Maybe.

Dad blinks, and for a minute I don't know if he can even see me. He's somewhere faraway. Somewhere I don't think I want to know about – but somewhere I *need* to know about, if we're going to make it through this.

Doing what you need to do, instead of what you want – another thing good parents do.

But I'm not a parent. I'm not Dad. I'm the kid. I'm just the kid. Why can't I just let this go? Why does it have to be me?

Useless questions. And time's wasting.

I touch Dad's shirt. It's all wet where he held me. "I got you wet," I say. Another lame thing. Everything I say is stupid. I can't help it. I think I've blown a few fuses through the course of the night.

Dad blinks. Touches his shirt. His pants, which are damp as well. He shakes his head. Then holds out the package. "I know this," he says.

The package is a small thing. About the size of a shoebox, completely covered in duct tape. On top of it – the side opposite the "truth will make you free" line – are two letters: "RR."

"What is it?"

"Few months ago there was a drug bust. Big one. New kind of drug."

"Red Rocks," I guess.

"Right. It's a designer MDPV."

"What's MDPV?"

Dad gives me a funny smile. "I can't tell you how much I love that you have to ask that, Mel." He takes out a knife. "It's a popular drug at raves. Makes people euphoric,

162

increases wakefulness and their ability to concentrate. Other than the fact that it makes them want to screw each other silly, have panic attacks, and go psychotic from time to time, it's awesome stuff." He stabs the packet. White powder spews out. "This is a new type of MDPV. Supposed to be much more potent. We seized almost thirty kilos. Thirty packages that looked just like this, full of stuff that looked just like this." He looks back at the hole I came out of a moment ago. It's full of water, spewing out not in a geyser but more in a small fountain, bubbling up and down in a two-foot surge with the ins and outs of the tide. "Whoever's smuggling it now must be using this as a drop point. Leaving drugs, picking up cash. It's a safe place, no one would go there normally."

"Holy cow. That's —" I break off as I realize something. "Wait, *we* seized almost thirty kilos? Do you mean 'we' like 'my fellow officers, or 'we' like 'me and my partner'?"

"Me. Linde. Zevahk. Knight." He grimaces. "And then there was that shootout a few months later."

"Are they connected?"

For a moment Dad looks unsure. Not like he doesn't know the answer. More like he's not even sure where he is. I worry for a second that I'm not the only person who blew a fuse or two. Maybe I'm not even the one whose fuses have blown the worst.

Then Dad's eyes lose focus. All of a sudden he's barely with me. Body present, but mind faraway in a memory that most would hide from forever. Not him. Not now.

The Ridealong

Sometimes memories warm us. Sometimes they burn. And Dad is braving the brightest flame.

"We got called in by Knight and Zevahk. They were doing a routine patrol. Heard shots fired. Found... found these dealers had a hostage... killed a kid. We provided backup. Me and Steve and Voss." His eyes come back to me, swimming back to Now from the horrible distance of a too-vivid Then. "The dealers were known providers of Red Rocks."

So we have Jack on the police bands. At least one dirty cop who tried to kill us earlier –

(*are they the same? is Jack the same person who shot at us from the police car? I don't think so, but is he?*)

– and it's all connected to a drug bust that turned into some kind of assassination.

Dad flings the remains of the Red Rocks package in his hands out into the waves. It froths, then sinks. There are going to be a lot of crazed fish in a few seconds.

He looks at it as it sinks.

The Ocean's Tomb moans.

Or maybe it's just me.

9

"What now?" Dad says. He's still looking at where he threw the box, full of a drug that people might be willing to die for – and will certainly kill for. "The truth will set you free."

I look around. We've got two dead bodies bashing around in a cave below our feet. An entire city of police convinced we're on a police-killing murder spree. And at least one bad cop them who wants to shut us up for reasons unknown.

A whiff of fish wafts up from the market below. I turn away. It's too rank, reminds me too much of the smell of the cave, the smell of Voss's body as it's being picked over by the busy little crab.

I look over the far side of the rocks, down the steep side opposite the fish market.

And see the car.

"Dad," I say.

He comes over to me. Looks at me like I'm looking at him: confused, worried.

Scared.

We climb down. Moving as fast as we can without tumbling head over heels down the slick, sharp stone. It's harder to go down than it was to come up. After all the banging around in the cave, the terror of seeing Voss, fight, the shock of nearly drowning… I can barely move my arms and legs. They feel far away, and I have to fight for every instant of control.

By the time we get to the bottom I'm shaking with exhaustion. Some of it's got to be a delayed shock reaction, too. Not every day you get to see a dead man in a cave under the ocean. And I got to see two. I even *caused* one of them.

Lucky me.

Dad puts an arm around me. His touch is so light I barely feel it, but I shake him off. "I'm okay," I say. A lie, and we both know it. But the important thing isn't that he believe me, it's that he keep moving. If we both stop, even for a moment, I think we might not start again. Sometimes movement – even blind, unthinking movement – is the only thing between you and despair.

Sometimes motion is a kind of counterfeit hope.

This is one of those times. We don't know what's going on. It looks bleak. But we'll keep moving. Keep moving.

I manage to straighten and start walking before Dad's gone two steps. I'm abreast of him almost instantly, and another second later I'm in front of him.

Then Dad's ahead. Running.

I didn't want to believe it. From the top of the rocks it was easy to fool myself. To say, "No, it's not *that* car."

But now, right on top of it... impossible to deny. There's the Darth Vader bobblehead sitting on the dash, the ripped passenger side seat, the small crack in the windshield.

Dad knows the car better than I do. But I know it well enough. Always parked away from the others when we go to the park for the Fourth of July barbecue, like the owner is afraid someone is going to maim his fifteen-year-old junker.

"This is...."

"Yeah," Dad says. And he finishes, because it has to be said. The words have to be said, because if they aren't they'll just hang there in the middle of the universe and drive us both mad.

If we're not already there.

"It's Knight's car."

10

Dad looks suddenly lost. Knight was how this all started: his dead body in the alley, his finger apparently having drawn our name in his own blood. We saw Knight's body, so how did the car get here? *Why* is it here?

So many questions. Not enough answers. And that lack of answers is going to kill us.

Or, at best, put us in jail forever.

Which reminds me. "Dad, call Jack."

Dad grimaces. "His Lordship?"

The joke is a weak one. Falls flat. But it's good to hear. When the jokes die, life isn't far behind. Laughter is the last, best defense against despair.

Of course, it's also just a socially acceptable alternative to running away shrieking at the top of your lungs. A lot of what we laugh at is gruesome, terrible when you really think about it. So maybe Dad's laugh *isn't* a good thing.

He clicks the button on his mic. "Jack, you there?"

"I'm here, Officer Latham. I'm always here. You should know that by now."

Dad looks at me. His eyebrows dance up to his hairline in the classic "What now?" position. I motion for him to give me the mic. He does. Doesn't even hesitate, and that makes me feel kinda warm, despite the circumstances. My dad's a cop. My dad's a good guy.

And my dad completely trusts me.

I click on. "I think I've figured you out, Jack."

"Oh?" His voice, always so expressive, sounds amused. He's smiling somewhere – probably somewhere close, since he always seems to know where we are and what we're doing. "Do tell."

"You love your kid, Jack?"

I'm going out on a limb. Way out. In fact, I'm basically dancing on a twig at this point. Right *or* wrong. If I'm wrong I might just piss him off for my assumption. If I'm right it might be much worse.

But we can't keep on going like this. We have to shake things up; turn them to our favor.

For maybe ten seconds he doesn't answer. And ten seconds isn't long when you're waiting for a movie to start or for a stoplight to change. When you're in a holding pattern at the door, hoping the guy of your dreams will kiss you, or when you're talking to a madman, hoping what you said won't be your end… ten seconds is forever.

He finally says, "Bravo, Melly Belly."

At the first word I think I have him. I figured it out. But the second two words change everything again. Because not even Liam knows –

(knew, *remember, he's dead and he doesn't know anything anymore just what it feels like to feel nothing at all*)

– that little pet name.

"How long have you been planning this?" I whisper.

"The whole month," says the voice on the other line. "Watching. Listening. Ever since your father and his friends killed my girl."

11

"This isn't about Red Rocks?" Dad says. He's finally getting it. Getting who Jack really is.

The kid in the alley. The innocent in the crossfire.

A scream from my dreams. A sound I know from what Dad has told me: "I'll kill you! I'll kill you all!"

Looks like someone's making good on the threat.

"Do you know who this is?" I ask Dad.

"I don't remember his name. I never got it, and the investigators from internal affairs kept me away from the files. I could maybe get it if I was at the station or had my MDT, but...."

"Right about now," said Jack, "you're probably discussing who I am, right? I mean, who I really am."

Neither of us answer. We both just look at the mic like Jack might reach through and kill us with a combination of bare hands and dark magic.

"Come now. Let's keep things civil. I ask, you answer. That's how polite conversation goes."

I hold out the mic to Dad. "Fine, what do you want to know?" he says.

"*Tsk, tsk.*" I can almost picture Jack shaking his head through the radio. "Put Mel back on. We were having such a good chat, after all. Besides, you're not ready for what I have to say." And then something dark creeps into his voice, which has until now been oh-so-pleasant. "Not yet, anway. But soon, Latham. Soon."

Dad hands the mic back to me.

Sure. No problem.

Sometimes having a dad who trusts you is a big pile of suck.

I click the mic. "Yeah, we're talking about who you are."

"Well, that's fine. You don't have your car, your computer. So that just leaves your father's memory, which is probably pretty spotty after everything that went down."

I can practically hear Dad's fists clench. I know he's thinking about the lost lives in the alley. About his partner, Linde, dying and him not being able to do anything about it.

"So are *you* going to tell us who you are? Who you really are?" I say.

The voice is silent again. Then: "Sure." I look at Dad. He's leaning forward so far I think he might topple over. Not just ears, but every *muscle* oriented on the words that are about to come from the radio.

It clicks. The voice: "I'm nobody."

I lift a shaking mic to my mouth. "What do you mean?"

"I used to be a man with a family. I used to be a father with a child. But now... I'm just a voice on the other side of darkness. I'm truth." He pauses. Another ten second slice of forever. "I'm the end."

The radio gives that telltale click that tells us it's off again. I still give it a try. "Jack?" No response. "Jack, what do you want us to do? What now? Jack?"

Nothing.

"What now?" I ask.

I'm still talking to Jack, but Dad is the one who answers. He looks at the car. "Go to the station. Hopefully we can get in and –"

"Are you *nuts*?" The words burst out before I can control them. And I don't think I would have stopped them even if I could. "That's suicide. The whole police force has got to be looking for us. We go there we're nailed."

"You got a better idea?" He almost snarls at me. I fall back a step or two.

"Yeah," I say. I don't, but my brain scrambles for something. All I can think is that I don't want Dad to go to jail. I don't want *me* to go to jail, either, but for a second I forget about myself. I just don't want him going to jail. If he ends up in jail, there'll be no coming back. Cops don't tend to last long or do too well when they get thrown in with the same people they've been putting away. And I don't want him leaving me.

Too many people have left me.

My brain finds something. "Zevahk," I say.

"What?"

"Let's go to one of them. Zevahk was there. At the shooting. Maybe he'll listen."

Dad waves the base of the radio around. "You really think Jack Be Nimble is going to let us get to them? He's got us on a string, and he knows it."

"It's better than nothing!" The words shriek out of me, so loud they drown out the moans of the Ocean's Tomb and the slamming surf at our back. Dad doesn't exactly fall back, but he does sort of shrink into himself for a moment.

"I.... Sorry," he finally manages. He passes a hand in front of his eyes, like he's trying to drop the curtain on the night. "I'm tired. Just so tired."

Then the hand falls away. His eyes shine, but they seem present, alert.

"Yeah. Let's go see him. Maybe he'll... maybe he'll help."

Dad turns, grabs the handle of the driver's side door. Then pauses, staring inside. "You wouldn't happen to know how to hotwire a 1999 POC, would you?" Then he snaps his fingers. "Knight kept a spare in the trunk, behind the lug wrench."

Dad leans in. Pops the trunk.

"You want me to drive?" I say, aware he's been awake and driving for something like fifteen or sixteen hours at this point.

"No. I'm good." He flashes me a smile that somehow makes me feel a little better. "Thanks, Melly. You're a good girl."

The little compliment is like a match in deep space. It doesn't get rid of the blackness, but it's something. A tiny spot of hope and warmth.

We go around back to get the key from the trunk.

And stop dead when we see what's back there.

12

I don't know how Jack crushed Zevahk into the trunk of Knight's car. Zevahk must weigh over two hundred pounds, and every inch of him is folded up on itself. The round body that looked like a weird blue sausage whenever he was crammed into his police uniform now just looks awkward and ugly now that he's crammed in the back of Knight's trunk.

Blood streams down the side of his head, over his closed eyes. A lake of the stuff has pooled on the mat of the trunk, drying into a sticky black-brown gunk.

"Is he...?" I can't say the word. The last word. The word that matters.

"I don't know." Dad leans in. "I think so." His voice hitches.

He touches Zevahk's neck, feeling for a pulse. "I can't...." He frowns. Not the frown of a man touching death. Just someone concentrating. "Maybe."

Then Zevahk's eyes pop open. I scream. So does he. Mine is wordless. A cry of terror, the shriek of a person who is looking at death come to life.

His cry is not wordless. His scream packs an entire world of sound and emotion into three small syllables. "I'm *SORRRRRRRYYYYYYYYYY!*"

His eyes are wild, spinning in their sockets like he's trapped in a dream, a nightmare. He sobs, gasps. Life surging out of him, then being yanked back as he sucks each breath into his lungs by force of will.

I realize that his face isn't the only thing bloodied. Everything on him is bent and bruised. His bones have been broken. Arms twisted, legs cracked so what should have had single joints in the middle now have multiple hinges.

One of his feet is twisted around so it faces completely backward. For some reason, that's the worst thing. I can't imagine what could have done it, or how much it must have hurt.

"Sorry... sorry... sorry... sorry...." Zevahk is saying the word with every breath now. Eyes still spinning sightlessly, still empty of everything.

No, that's wrong. There's something there. He's insane.

And that's true. He's gone mad. Whoever put him in this car also pushed him to a place so far beyond reality that I don't know if he'll ever come back.

"Sorry... sorry...."

"Zevahk," says Dad. He's looking around the man like he wants to help but doesn't know where to start. How do you do first aid on a guy who looks like he was put through a machine press before being compacted into the trunk of a car? I've crushed aluminum cans that looked better than Zevahk does.

"Sorry... sorry... sorry...."

Dad reaches for Zevahk. "Who did this to you, buddy?"

"Sorry... *sorry... SORRY!*"

Zevahk's cries raise in volume the closer Dad's hands come. To the point I worry the guy is going to burst whatever blood vessels are still whole in his body and die right there.

I don't know if I can handle another dead body.

Dad seems to think the same thing. His hands go back. "We'll get you some help, Z."

He looks at me with a strange expression. Lost, like he doesn't know what to do.

I feel strangely angry at that. Dads aren't supposed to look like he does now. They're *always* supposed to know what to do. That's what makes them "Dad" instead of "some guy I live with."

"Sorry... sorry...."

Zevahk's words begin to gurgle. Like he's drowning right here, like the waves that end a good hundred feet away have somehow found their way into his lungs.

"Hold on, Z." Dad snaps back to himself. Knows what to do again. Apparently decides that he's got to get his friend to a hospital, however he has to do it. He leans in and pops the hatch that holds the lug wrench and jack behind it.

The car's spare key is taped to the lug wrench. Dad twists it away. Then puts a hand on the trunk. I realize he's going to slam it shut, slam Zevahk inside there, alone and drowning inside himself.

"Sorry... sorry...."

It seems wrong.

"Sorry... sorry...."

It's also the only thing we can do. He's not going to let us touch him. He's dying.

"Sorry…"

His voice weakens.

And the first shot takes him in the throat.

13

Stories are full of heroes who stand fast. Who rise up in a hail of bullets, draw their own guns, and strike down evildoers in an instant.

Well, I guess I'm no hero. I see Zevahk's throat tear open and know he's dead. Just a last few sounds as the breath rasps out of his body.

"Sorry... sorr...."

In that instant I hit the ground. I slam myself down so hard the breath whooshes out of me in an explosion almost as loud as the next bullet.

Zevahk goes silent.

Dad screams, "Honey!" from beside me.

"I'm fine!"

I see where the shot came from. A cruiser is parked nearby. Probably came up on us while our attention was focused on Zevahk –

(*Dead. Zevahk's dead. Knight and Voss and Liam and now Zevahk and when will it stop oh please let it stop!*)

– then opened fire. I don't know whether the shooter meant to kill Zevahk or was simply aiming at us. Doesn't matter. It just matters that we are in trouble.

I can see Dad reach for his gun. He wears a Glock 22, .40 caliber load. That's the gun I've shot on the range. It's a good gun, one of the most popular guns for law enforcement across the U.S. Partly that's because it uses an ammo they like. Partly because it's supposed to be pretty much indestructible.

But no matter how good a gun you own, it won't help you a bit if it's just not there.

Where'd it go? Where's his gun?

Dad's hand slaps the empty holster where his gun was – I *know* it was there – earlier in the night. But now it's gone. How, and where?

Jack, of course. It has to be Jack. How he did it I have no idea. But it was him.

I suddenly think of Dad, lifting the card key off the attendant at the Moo Cow carpark, and wonder if Jack somehow did something like that to Dad's gun. When? How?

Doesn't matter. Not at the moment. What matters now is that we're facing someone with who just killed a man, who is still firing at us, and Dad has nothing more than a collapsible baton – assuming *that's* still on his belt.

The shooter in the cruiser – parked in the road just beyond the beach, maybe a hundred feet away – lets out a flurry of shots. Some ping into metal, others hit with dry thuds into the sand around the car. Some make a meaty sound that I figure is Zevahk – what's left of him.

I realize I'm screaming.

The gun shooting at us is louder than the one Dad has. This has to be the M4. A big gun, so even if Dad had his own sidearm, we'd be seriously outgunned.

Dad says something. It seems to take a long time to wend its way through the gunfire, the panic, the air itself.

"Get ready."

Ready for *what*? my mind screams.

The M4 pounds away as he does, the bullets flying around us like a swarm of hornets, stingers extended, more deadly than any other species.

Dad yanks me away.

Back toward the Ocean's Tomb.

14

Going up before was scary. This time it's a nightmare. I know Dad's right: it's the only way to go. The others lead only to empty space (suicide), the ocean (Dad can't swim with his rig or his vest, and no time to strip them off), or straight into the arms of the guy with the M4.

So up the rocks we go.

Bullets keep zipping past. Keep pinging off the rocks. I feel one hit near me. Feel chips of rock explode into my face. My eyes close fast enough to keep me from being blinded, but it's close. I feel blood flow down my nose and cheek, a million tiny cuts opened as the volcanic rock splits into shards of glass.

We climb. Fingers bleeding, knuckles split. Feet slipping.

I hear something below us. Know it's *him*. The man who's following – trying to kill us. I know he won't give up.

We climb.

The top of the rocks seemed big before, when we were looking for some unknown clue as to where to go.

This time it seems bigger. Massive. Certainly big enough that by the time we pick our way over the top, get to the far side and start down, the killer cop will be up there as well. Then there's nowhere to go. He'll draw, he'll fire.

Then it'll be over. No way a trained shooter misses with a long gun at this range.

We're dead.

Dad seems to know it, too. He pulls out his collapsible baton. Flicks it open and motions for me to get behind him.

I do, but I'm not waiting for him to fight. That's suicide. I don't want us to die, I'm not willing to just give up – even if giving up comes in the form of a last, brave charge to certain death.

And then I see our way out. Wonder if it's maybe worse than the M4.

Don't think. Do it.

"Dad," I whisper. "Come on."

I yank him away from the edge of the rocks. Toward the center of the mass. The two jets keep shooting out as the rock mountain moans. Between the jets: the fountain where I almost died.

And that's where I'm headed.

We get there, and I explain what I think we should do. Dad looks at me like I'm crazy. I think he's probably right.

"You got any better ideas?" I demand. I hope he does. *Pray* he does.

He doesn't.

The hole the water is gushing out of isn't wide enough for two people to escape through, even without the water spewing from it.

But near the top? Maybe we can both fit.

We maneuver ourselves into the foamy water. Salt stings my eyes. Gets up my nose. I try to hold my breath, but all I manage is a choking gasp. I hear Dad snorting beside me as well.

Then we almost fall together. Grabbing one another as we pitch into the hole. Hands reaching for the sides, knowing that to go too far is to die.

We stop waist-deep in the hole. Our heads are in the water, which still fountains out waist-high.

I lean back, pushing my back as far as it will bend. Eyes screwed shut. I breathe in, ready to start choking and drowning.

I don't. I can breathe. It's unpleasant, my lips curled back over clenched teeth so as to filter as much of the falling water as possible, like I'm in the world's heaviest rainfall. But I can do it.

Beside me, I hear Dad doing the same, hear his sputtering breath.

Now we just have to wait here and hope the gunman doesn't see us in the thick column of water. If he does, or if he thinks to look around the back of the column to where we're leaning out, we're dead.

And then I hear the sound of footsteps.

He's on top of the rocks.

He's up here with us.

And I can hear him coming toward us. Our luck – if you can call it that – has finally run out.

15

I feel Dad's hand on mine. Gripping hard. I hold him back. A wordless conversation.

Him: *He's here.*

Me: *I know.*

Him: *Stay.*

Me: *Where would I go?*

Then the pulses on my hand turn into a steady grip. A feel I interpret as, *Wait.*

I do.

Wait.

The footsteps are close. So close I can hear the rasp-scrape of leather boots making their way over sand- and salt-covered rocks.

Wait.

Darkness all around, darkness approaching. Still near-choking on water and my own fear.

Wait.

Then Dad gently pulls on me. I drag in a final gagging breath. Then we're both in the column of water. Fully and completely.

The water in here is dark. It seems saltier than normal seawater. Could be my imagination, or maybe it's got something to do with being filtered through the rock.

Whatever it is, my eyes burn. I shut them for a second, but open them quickly.

I have to see.

No details. Everything is wavy, shattered. Broken in a million million pieces by the million million individual water droplets that make up our hiding space. We are in plain view, hidden while standing only feet from our pursuer.

I see him. Blurred, shifting as the water burbles around me. He is nothing but a dark smear across the black night. A tall creature come calling, a monster come to claim us here, alone under the stars.

I'm holding my breath again. I resolve never to go swimming again as long as I live.

The man moves slowly. Looking over the front side of the rocks, where surf crashes against it.

I can't hold on much longer.

I lean out. Dad's hand grabs for me, but I'm on the verge of panic. If I don't breathe, I'll die.

I see the man. Leaning over the front of the rock pile, holding a huge gun that I guess is the M4.

His back is to me. All I see is the gun and the uniform blues.

He starts to lean back around toward me.

I whip myself back into the column.

The dark shape moves toward the fountain. Toward the place where Dad and I clutch each other under our blanket of water. It stops right in front of the column. Shifts its weight. I can't tell if it's staring at us or looking somewhere else.

It moves away. To the other side of the rock pile.

Dad and I lean out. Gasping silently, trying to gulp as much air as possible without making a sound.

We hear the man start down, start back toward his car.

We climb silently out of the hole.

I put my hand down. Pull myself out. Only the whisper of the water. Nothing that can be heard over the moaning Tomb.

Then I kick a rock. It slides over the side of another rock. Disappears into a crevice with an echo that shatters the silence.

Dad is on his knees beside me. We both freeze. Every part of our minds focused solely on hearing, on listening for telltale sounds that might indicate our pursuer heard the noise; that he's coming back.

Nothing.

Dad stands.

And we hear something – someone – scrambling back up toward us.

We run for the far side of the mountain and throw ourselves over.

16

I roll. Feel more cuts open. My hands go out to stop my fall. I force them in, close to my body.

The human body isn't designed to fall with acceptance. Pitching headfirst into gravity's embrace is something that we fight with outstretched arms, with legs desperately trying to get themselves below us. It happens without conscious thought. And it's what I need *not* to happen right now. Screw climbing. Screw even the concept of a controlled fall.

We have to roll down.

But reality sets in halfway down. If I don't stop bouncing I'm going to die. Or at least break a bone, which amounts to the same thing when you have an insane gunman after you.

Dad falls with me, into me. I feel his arms around me for part of the drop, protecting me.

Doesn't work.

My hands fling out again. Trying to stop the freefall, turn it into something slower, safer. They hit rock. Already-split knuckles cry protests as they break open still further. There is no thought, only pain.

One of my hands catches something. My shoulder feels like it's been wrenched out of its socket, but I stop my death-tumble.

Beside me, Dad stops as well. Gasping raggedly.

We don't look up. Don't have time. We climb down almost as fast as we fell. Because we can hear the sound of someone climbing after us. Not insane – there's no sliding sand, no pounding of flesh against rock that would indicate he's falling like we did.

But he's coming fast.

And he's armed.

Then we're down.

Dad grabs my hand. We run through sand. Back to the fish market. The maze of empty kiosks and stalls that have been boarded over for the night.

I realize how dark it is. How alone and lonely I feel. Dad's beside me, but utterly silent. I might as well be the only person in the world. Just me and the man behind, the man who wants to kill me.

We dash between the stalls, turning this way and that. Some of the stalls have flaps that extend over to the next stall, awnings that meet in the center to create makeshift roofs that protect from the elements – sun most of the year, rain on those rare wet days. They make me feel like I'm running through tunnels, through deep places.

The fish market is paved, so the sand can't grip us, can't yank us back and keep us from our top speed. But the slap of feet on sidewalk will give our position away.

We hear the *smack-smack-smack* of our pursuer's rapid steps. I think I can hear him breathing, winded from the pursuit. Probably my imagination. Or maybe not. No way to be sure.

Dad turns. Drags me behind one of the kiosks. Motions me to be quiet with a finger to his lips.

We both listen. I pull his shirt sleeve – still wet – and point to our left. I think that's where I hear him coming from. The footsteps are softer now. He's slowed down. Looking for us. Hunting us. I can picture him, eyes scanning up and down the rows of stalls, searching for us as he walks. Cat and mouse, predator and prey.

Dad waits, a long moment. Nods. We creep around the stall we're hunched beside. Trying to time our movements with the motion of the wind, the flaps of canvas awnings and tie-downs all around us.

We dash across an aisle. Open to sight in four directions at once.

I see him.

Again his face is turned away. Bad, because I want to know who he is. *Need* to know. Who he is will tell us what's going on – maybe how to survive it.

But if I saw him, he'd see us, too. He's that close. And he's still got that M4, holding it like he means business – which I know he does.

Then we're past, squatting behind the next kiosk, waiting for him to pass a bit further.

His footsteps stop abruptly. He starts running. Feet fast and hard across the pavement. *Slap-slap-slap-slap.*

I don't know if he saw something. Maybe a shadow out of the corner of his eye. Maybe he heard the scrape of our shoes on the cement, the sound of our ragged breathing. Maybe he just *knew*, the way monsters know when you're in your bed, blanket over your head and terrified to look out.

He's coming for us.

I move first this time. Yanking Dad with me. Both of us fleeing in time, our footsteps perfectly matched as we run.

I wonder what I'd look like crammed in a trunk like Zevahk. Splayed out across an alley like Knight. Shoved in a cave –

(*crab scuttling across my eye and I'm dead we're both dead we can't escape we're dead all dead now*)

– like Voss.

"No."

Not sure if I actually say the word, or if it just bounces around the jumbled furniture of my mind. Either way, it gives me a bit of strength. Pushes me away from the sudden despair that threatens to swallow me.

I'm not going to end up like those guys. I'm *not*. Dad and I will find out what's going on. Will figure out how to end it. To make it right.

Suddenly that is my entire existence. I don't care about school, about friends. Don't even care about survival for its own sake.

I want justice. For Dad's partner. For Voss, Knight, and Z.

For Liam.

I am outpacing Dad. I grab him. Yank him with me. Ridiculous, a girl pulling a big man. But he stumbles along a bit faster.

Still in the fish market. Still hearing that *slap-slap-slap* behind us. Only now it's faster. *Slapslapslapslap*, the shoes coming down so fast and hard I half expect them to kick the world right out of orbit.

I pull Dad to the right. Another right. Another.

The cop is on our tail. *Slapslapslap.*

Another right. Moving in a big circle. Looking for something. Anything. A way to hide, a way to fight.

Nothing. We can't leave the market – the maze of stalls is our only cover. We have to....

I spot a hope. Pull Dad with me again. He doesn't resist. He trusts.

I hope that trust won't kill us.

17

One of the stalls isn't a perfect square. There's a notch in it, an area where people can get out of the crowd to get drinks or napkins or condiments or something. Just a little space, maybe four feet by four feet. Barely enough to hold my dad and I standing together. And if we're in there we'll be easily seen. Sitting ducks.

I go there. Dad pulls back. Resists. I look at him. Hope my face says what I want it to: *Trust me.*

He does. And, again, I hope I'm not killing us with this move.

We cram ourselves into the stall. And as we do I reach down and grab the knife Dad used to cut up the Red Rocks package. Flip it open with a *snick* that's so loud it's like a lightning strike in my ears. It may be my imagination but it seems to make the pursuing feet move even faster – *slapslapslaslasla...*

I slash a pair of tie-downs. The third doesn't want to cut.

Slapslap... the feet are right around the corner...

... one more desperate cut...

... I hear feet scraping around a turn...

... he'll see us...

... the rope I'm cutting parts...

... *slapslapslap...*

... and the canvas awning flutters down. Covers Dad and me from head to toe. I hope it looks like a cover laying flat against the perfect box of a stall. Hope the killer doesn't think of examining it too closely. Hope our feet aren't sticking out.

Slapslapslapsla –

The footsteps stop abruptly. Not right in front of us, but very close. Somewhere in the same aisle.

I can picture the guy, looking at the stall. "That's not right," he's thinking. Pulling out the M4, aiming it and making sure he won't miss. Maybe taking a step toward us to create an absolutely perfect shot.

The feet take a step. My stomach twists painfully. I have to concentrate on not running screaming out of our hiding place.

Dad's hand grabs mine. Like he knows exactly what I'm thinking – maybe because he's thinking it, too – and is trying to keep me from making a move that will kill us both.

Our pursuer doesn't move for a long time. Probably listening, and I'm suddenly gripped by the conviction that he can hear my heartbeat. It's thundering through my body, individual gunshots booming through my ears in time with my pulse.

He has to hear that. He has *to.*

But he doesn't. There's just the wind.

He moves. I hear footsteps. Not running, but moving stealthily. Still trying to flush us out, to catch us running away.

The blood still pounds through my head, but other than that all I hear is his footsteps and the slap-crack of canvas and nylon in the wind.

Too late, I realize my mistake. Realize that I let the awning fall over us, but didn't anchor it at all. Didn't hold onto it.

I reach, but I'm too late. The wind flips it up, flapping it like a curtain, completely revealing us.

I see him as he turns a corner. M4 tucked into a shoulder, extended past him as he keeps up the hunt. I still don't see a face.

We wait as the canvas falls back over us. Covers and protects us. I think if it were up to me we'd just wait there forever. The next morning the stall's owner would open up to find me and Dad there, shivering with terror and wondering if we were about to be saved or slaughtered.

Dad's hand, holding mine, squeezes once. He reaches out and peels back the canvas that covered us. Looks around. Then he pulls us in the opposite direction from where the hunter went.

Back toward the rocks. Toward the Tomb.

I know what Dad is thinking. I know, and it makes sense. But I hate it. I don't know if I can do it.

We're weaponless, on foot. Sooner or later we're going to be discovered, and then killed.

So we have to get back to the one avenue of escape. Knight's car.

Dad leads me back to the Tomb. The moans are definitely coming from me now. My entire body is screaming, on fire. I can barely move – how am I supposed to climb?

Then I see Dad. His face is cut. His forehead and cheeks bloody. His hands run red. He hasn't complained, hasn't so much as murmured. He just wants to get away. To save me.

So if he can do that... then I guess I can, too. He'll save me, I'll save him. We'll wake up from this nightmare, and we'll be a family again.

Up we go.

Over.

Down.

My body hates me for this. Every inch is agony. Every second one that I expect to be shot from behind.

But we aren't. We make it. We get away, we get to the car.

Dad goes to the trunk. Zevahk is still there, broken body now riddled with the bullets that found their way into the small space. His eyes stare into a forever-place that seems oddly enticing. At least restful.

I'm so tired.

Dad closes Zevahk's eyes. Then closes the trunk. He does it as quietly as possible, but one of the hinges was bent in the firefight and it squeaks as Dad lowers it. It sounds deafening in the night. So does the click of the latch – loud as a gunshot.

We both look toward the Tomb. I figure our pursuer will be there, standing at the base, sighting down the barrel of the M4. Two quick shots. Checkmate.

But there's no one.

Dad gets in the car. So do I.

He starts the car. It turns over just fine.

We drive away.

I inhale. And wonder how long it's been since I breathed. It feels like forever.

I wonder how long I'm going to *keep* breathing.

18

I don't know how long we drive. Forever. A day, a week, a month. I'm tempted to look over at the fuel gauge to see if we have enough gas to just drive... *away*. Somewhere far enough that no one has ever heard of me or Dad or anyone we know. Somewhere we can disappear, if we haven't already.

It feels like we're fading, losing ourselves in whatever Jack has planned, and whatever else we're caught up in. And those are two different things, I think: there's Jack, who has his game, his plans for us. Then there's whoever shot Zevahk, whoever's been following us in the police car all night. I don't think they're the same person – even if they might be looking for the same final outcome: me and my dad dead.

I want to look at that gas gauge. But I don't. Because as soon as I look the fuel level will read "E" and we'll be worse off than before. That's how these things work.

We don't need to stop right now. Stopping in a city full of police who are all looking for you? Bad idea.

Of course, *everything* is a bad idea now. Go home? That's sure to be crawling with detectives, with CSI guys. Those nerds aren't like the ones in the TV shows. They can't really tell your whole life story from a single hair. But they are smart, and a lot of them are armed. So we don't want to go there.

And as much as I want to just drive away, that won't solve much. Short of going to Mexico, we're going to have to deal with this mess at some point.

Dad's radio clicks on. "You having fun?" says Jack.

Dad doesn't bother with niceties. He snatches the mic. "What the hell are you doing this for, you sonofabitch? I'm sorry you lost your kid. So, what, you're going to take mine away from me? Is that how this works? That was passes for justice in that sick mind of yours?"

He's almost shrieking with rage, and the sound of his voice is so very loud in Knight's little car.

Jack laughs. Long and loud and hearty. He could be trying out for a position as a mini-mall Santa. Just ho-ho-hoing us along as we turn down one dark street after another.

His laughter finally slows; I swear I can hear him wiping tears away. "I love it," he says. "I *absolutely love it.*"

Dad holds the mic against his lips like he's going to say something. I guess he changes his mind. He drops it away from his face. His teeth grind so hard I can see the muscles in his jaw and temple bouncing up and down. The lights in the dashboard cast weird shadows against his face. He looks pale, worn.

Dead.

That sense of fate takes hold of me again. I feel like I'm looking at a ghost. A spirit who simply hasn't clued to the fact that he needs to move on. Chills sweep through me, and they have nothing to do with my still-soaked clothes.

Jack speaks, and now his voice has no laughter in it. Nothing even approaching mirth. "Listen up, Latham. I'm not done with you. And until I am, you're not going to fully understand what the point of this is. But I can assure you of this: your daughter is going to leave you. Your friends will leave you. When I'm done, your life will leave you." Jack is panting with excitement. He sounds like a wild animal. A rabid dog. "*All* your lives will end, there or not, ready or not, here I come." And he laughs laughs laughs.

The rage falls away from Dad's expression, leaving it strangely slack. Then he glances at me. And the love, the fear on his face leave me breathless. "Please," he whispers. "I really don't care what you do to me. I won't fight it. I'll *let* it happen. Just… please leave Mel out of it."

"Leave her out of it?" Jack laughs again. But not a Santa laugh this time. This time it's Jack Frost – cold and completely merciless. It freezes my blood, leaves me shivering. "She's already in it, Latham. Has been since before this night began. And she can't leave until it's over."

A long moment passes. All I can hear is the whisper of air passing along the outside of the car, the hum of tires on asphalt.

Then Jack says, "But don't worry, it'll be over soon."

Then the radio clicks and we're on our own. Driving who-knows-where. But wherever we go, whatever we choose, I think we'll be doing exactly what he wants us to.

Whoever he really is, whatever he really wants, Jack is in control. He has been since the beginning. Since, as he said, *before* the beginning.

All we can do is play along, and hope the game ends well for us.

PART FIVE:
A PEEK BEHIND THE CURTAIN

```
June 30
PD Property Receipt - Evidence
Case # IA15-6-3086
Rec'd: 6/29
Investigating Unit: IA/Homicide
```

JOURNAL
DAY TWENTY-NINE

Liam is still calling. At least, I think it's him. He calls and hangs up without saying anything.

Dad was cleared in the inquiry. He goes back to work tomorrow.

I can't let that happen. He'll die the next time something like this happens, I know it.

I just <u>know it</u>.

1

Dad keeps turning. I wonder how many of the turns are random, how many of them are designed to avoid the roadblocks and stops that have probably gone up to look for us.

"What now?" I ask.

Dad shakes his head. "I don't know. I just don't want anything to happen to you."

But it already has. Things have happened to me tonight, things that I know he's going to beat himself up about forever. And that's part of what makes him a good dad, too: he wants to protect me from everything, but never can. And even if he could, I think he wouldn't – we have to get out into the thick of it. Be hurt once in a while. That's the only way to learn, to grow.

But it still cuts him up inside when it happens to me.

Suddenly, I realize where we should be headed. Not out of the pain, but into it. We can't escape, so we'll have to embrace.

At the least, maybe we can help someone else this way.

"Dad, we have to go to Glenn."

"What?" He blinks. "Why?"

"He's the only one who hasn't been killed or hurt."

"What do you mean?"

I can tell by his expression that Dad's already decided I'm speaking out of panic. I have to head that off – I know what I said is right. We have to get to Glenn, and we have to get to him fast.

"Hear me out, Dad. There were a bunch of you the day of the bust. And the only one who hasn't been hit yet is Glenn."

Dad shakes his head. "No, Glenn wasn't there, I told you that. He was out sick. And besides, I *was* there and I haven't been killed."

"No, but Jack's making us miserable. And he said your life would end. So maybe he's toying with you because you wanted to run out and save his kid but didn't. Maybe he's making you suffer for that, before...." I can't end that sentence. I switch back to the original point of my thought. "But Glenn – he was out sick, fine, but he was Voss's partner. So he *should* have been there, and he wasn't. If he had been there, had been doing his job, maybe he could have helped. Maybe he could have changed something." I pause to let that sink in. "At least, I bet that's how Jack will see it. He doesn't strike me as a guy who will say, 'You're off the hook because you weren't there.' He's into punishment more than forgiveness."

Dad is silent. He purses his lips. "Maybe."

Fate reaches fingers into my mind. Pulls at me. "For sure. Jack said 'there or not, ready or not.' Like, 'whether you were there that day or not.' Dad, we have to get to him. Fast. What if Jack gets to him first?"

Dad looks at me. "What if the killer gets to *you* first?"

I smile. Try to, at least. "I'll stay in the car where it's safe. I'm just a ridealong, after all."

Dad doesn't smile back. After a moment my smile fades as well. Because I can feel that things are winding down. Things are coming to a close.

We're going to find out what Jack wants. And find out if we get to live or die at the end of his game.

2

The ride to Glenn James's house seems like it takes only a few minutes. But dawn is reaching fingers of light across the horizon by the time we get to his subdivision.

All night? How has it been all night?

Finding Knight, going to the bar and Liam... the nightmare at the Ocean's Tomb. It's all a blur of colors and sounds, like something you'd see from the Tilt-a-Whirl at a carnival. Just hints with enough detail to figure out what you're seeing without *actually* seeing it. And it's enough to make you dizzy and sick and about halfway through the ride maybe you wish you could get off.

I definitely wish I could get off this ride, that's for sure.

Glenn's house, like his family, seems perfect. It's light yellow, with perfectly-mown grass, flowers planted all around the outside, and a real-as-I'm-standing-here-now white picket fence surrounding the whole thing. I've been here twice, and both times I had a great time but also felt a bit jealous that it wasn't *my* house. That Dad and I didn't have a Mrs. James of our own. That Mom died before giving me any little brothers or sisters.

Life's a drag, huh.

The place seems cheery even in the early-morning twilight. Catching the predawn glimmers and throwing them back a hundred times stronger, standing as a beacon of order and goodness in the middle of a world gone bad.

I want in. I want in that world so badly, and I wonder for a moment if the reason I urged Dad to come here was less about what's happening to us and more just the need to see this place again.

Dad goes to the door. Hammers on it. Three sharp raps, *one-two-three*. The sound of a cop knocking, which is pretty unmistakable. You don't even have to hear, "Police, please open the door!" after hearing that knock – you just *know* who's outside.

There's a long stretch of nothing, then the door swings wide.

Glenn stands there in boxers and a t-shirt. His hair is mussed, and he's blinking blearily, like he hasn't quite woken up yet. When he sees Dad and me, though, he stops blinking and starts staring.

"Holy Mary," he says. "What the hell happened to you?"

"You mind?" Dad says, gesturing inside the house. "It's a bit cold out here."

"No," says Glenn. "I mean – no, of course not."

He moves aside to let us pass.

Dad walks ahead of me, then turns as Glenn closes the door behind us.

"What's going on?" says Glenn. "You all right?"

"No," says Dad. "Neither are you."

"What do you mean by *that*?" asks Glenn.

"Where's your wife, the girls?" asks Dad.

"They're at my in-laws. They go every year for a week." He smiles a tight smile. "I get to live the life of a bachelor: pizza rolls and beer for breakfast, lunch, and dinner." The smile disappears. "Now you going to tell me what this is about?"

"I think you're in danger," says Dad. "Someone's killing off the guys in our unit."

"What do you mean, someone's –"

"What do you think I mean?" Dad almost roars. He has to visibly get himself under control. "Knight, Voss, and Zevahk are dead."

Glenn's gaze seems to wobble strangely. "No, that's not possible. I mean –" Then it steadies out and he grins a real grin: wide, with dimples at the corners. "Haha, Latham. Very funny. Is there a stripper on the way, too?" He turns and heads toward the back of the house. "Come on back, I'll get you a drink and you can explain why April Fool's has come at such a weird time this year."

Dad looks at me. "It's true," I say. "They're all gone. So is Liam."

Glenn turns back to look at us. "Liam?"

"Sarge's kid. He…." I swallow. "He killed himself."

This time the wobble isn't confined to Glenn's gaze. Something about my words must convince him this isn't a joke. He weaves on his feet, almost leaning into a nearby wall. "No. Sarge's kid? He's not…."

"Believe it, Glenn," says Dad. "I saw it myself."

"Now *I* need a drink," says Glenn. He turns and walks down a short hall that leads to the kitchen. We follow.

Dad stops in the doorway. I nearly collide with him.

"I thought you said the girls and your wife were on vacation," says Dad.

"Yeah," says Glenn.

"So why are there two glasses on the table?"

That's when I feel the gun poke into my ribs.

3

We're too late.

Too late to save Knight. Voss. Zevahk.

Liam.

Always too late.

I turn, and see the other guy from the Exxon. And now I know who I killed in the cave, because this one is still wearing the red flannel shirt with "Ray" written on a pin.

I must have killed Bob. Knowing his name makes what happened in the cave worse. Makes it more real. A dead man with no name is barely there. No more reality to him than a statistic on a news report. But "Bob" is a person with friends and family and a life – no matter how badly lived.

Ray me with the gun again pushing me into the kitchen. And looks at Glenn. "You let 'em in, you dumbass?"

Glenn shrugs. "I was asleep. It's five in the morning. And the whole point of you and your brother following was to make sure there were no problems." He pauses, then adds with a delicious grin, "Dumbass."

Ray's look hardens further. Not just angry at us now, but at Glenn.

Dad looks dumbstruck. "Glenn?" he says. He sounds like a little kid. Lost. Alone.

Glenn shrugs. "Business, Latham. It's always been about business." He looks over our shoulders at Ray. "You might as well do it in here." He sighs and looks around at his immaculately clean kitchen. "At least the tile's easier to clean than the carpet in the living room."

4

Dad and I are moving as one the instant Glenn says "clean." Even so, we're not fast enough to stop the first shot. It goes off with a tremendous explosion and I feel one of the now-familiar wasp-buzzes fly past my head. Something burns my ear and I feel blood flow down the side of my neck.

I don't cry out. Don't even make a sound. Survival has consumed me. When we came out of the caves a million years ago, when we climbed out of the trees in the jungle and made towns and began wearing suits and dresses and talking about stocks and bonds instead of berries and beasts, we pretended we were civilized. But it turns out there's a wildness buried inside us. It's deep, it sleeps while we hustle about our lives and Snapchat and Vine ourselves into oblivion.

But when it still can – still does – wake when truly needed.

I throw myself on Ray. Dad powers into him at the same time. We fight together, fight like we have practiced for this moment all our lives. Fists raining down in perfect sync. Legs kicking out like they are under joint control.

Glenn twists. Grabs Dad's right arm. I break the hold. Punch his throat. He gags. Dad buries a hand in his gut. Glenn tries to vomit and gag at the same time. Does a little dance that would have been comical in other circumstances.

Glenn goes down. We follow him. Pounding. Kicking. Punching.

My teeth are bared. At his throat. I have a moment where a now-distant part of me – the part that still remembers what it was like to have family and friends and a meaning in life – wonders if I can really do this.

The second shot goes off. I feel Dad shudder beside me.

5

"DAD!"

My teeth unlock, my muscles stop their motion. I'm locked in the dream. In the conviction I have that I will never see him again. That this is all leading up to the terrible moment when family ends, when we lose each other forever.

I feel warmth on my hands.

I feel death come to call. Just like my dream. My nightmares.

"DAD!" I scream it again. Then, a whisper. As though I can reel his soul back to his body with a near-silent prayer. "Please, Dad."

"I won't. I'm okay."

It takes a moment for the words to penetrate. To realize the shudder I felt wasn't him after all. The gunshot drove not up, but down.

Ray coughs. Blood comes out of his mouth.

"What's... what's going on?" he says. He looks genuinely confused. "Why are you... why are you...?"

He dies.

Another corpse. But this is one I can't quite bring myself to care about. I care more about the blood that spatters on my hands than I do about the soul it represents.

Then I realize we've left someone at our backs.

Dad and I spin.
Glenn.
He's smiling.
Holding a knife.

6

Most murders are committed with guns.

Knives are too personal. Too close. If you shoot someone you don't have to feel their blood on you, don't have to look in their eyes as the life leaves them.

But from the look on Glenn's face, I can see he *wants* to feel our blood. He *wants* to watch the lights flee our eyes.

Instead, though, we watch as something flickers in his own expression.

I look down. His gaze follows. He frowns. "When did that happen?" He looks back up. His expression is nearly amused. A "well, if that doesn't just beat all" kind of look.

The first shot – the one that took a notch out of my ear – continued past me and buried itself in his gut. Red stains the front of his t-shirt in a widening circle.

"Dammit," he mutters. His gaze wavers. Then he fixates on us. On me. "You killed me," he says.

And leaps forward. Knife outstretched. Intention clear: to take us with him. Because evil is like that. Evil doesn't want to simply destroy, it wants to make everyone as miserable and hurt as itself.

I see that evil hurtling at me. Knife pointed at my chest.

And I don't move.

7

We took Ray down without hesitation. But now, with Glenn coming toward me, I can't move.

I always wanted his wife to be my mother. Wanted his daughters to be my sisters.

How can I do anything to hurt him?

How can I run from him?

How can this be *real*?

And all that aside, my body is finally realizing what just happened with Ray. Adrenaline pulses through me so hard it's like my body doesn't even belong to me. All I can do is twitch as Glenn rushes me.

Then he slams backward as something hits him in the shoulder. I don't even hear the explosion. It's buried in the moment, in the surreality of it all.

I hear the second one, though. The moment when Dad pulls the trigger of Ray's gun. The moment when a hole – surprisingly small – opens above Glenn's right eye.

The knife drops from his hand.

He falls.

It's over.

Dad holds me.

I cry.

"It's over, baby," he says. "They can't hurt us, Melly Belly."

I don't even mind that he calls me that. Not one bit.

8

We leave the kitchen.

Two dead bodies, leaning against opposite walls with legs splayed out in front of them as though they're not dead at all but rather friends just lounging and chatting after a long time apart. It's gruesome and unreal and at the same time all too absolute and sickeningly *true*.

We walk out of the kitchen.

Through the living room.

I want to leave the house.

Dad senses it. Knows without me saying.

"I have to call this in. We have to explain now. We'll be able to."

I nod.

We leave. Stand in the driveway. I lean on Glenn's car. He has a nice Mustang. Cherry red. I keep circling the thought that he'll never drive it again. Behind it is a brown truck with a lift kit that I'm guessing belongs to the late and unlamented Ray.

Dad activates his mic. "Twenty fifty-five, calling dispatch."

I press harder into the Mustang. The metal is cool against my back. It feels good.

"Twenty fifty-five." Dad fiddles with a dial. "Twenty fifty-five, come in, dispatch." Nothing comes out of the radio.

I try not to care. Try to focus on the cool that's spreading down my frame, counteracting the overheat my body went through inside. The Mustang. I want it to be my world.

"Twenty fifty-five."

The Mustang.

The truck....

I jerk upward. "Dad –"

"Twenty fifty-five, please –"

I put a hand on his arm. Shake it. "Dad, where's the other car?"

He doesn't seem to notice me for a moment. "Why won't it work?" he says to himself. Then looks up. "Other car?"

"Glenn's Mustang is here. Ray showed up in a truck. We came in Knight's car." I point at each vehicle as I name them off. "Where's the cop car? Where's the person who's been shooting at us all night?" When Ray and Glenn tried to kill us, I thought that Glenn must have been the guy following us around all night. But then... then the cop car would have been here. He would have *had* to leave it here.

So where is it?

And at that moment, lights wash over us.

A cop car.

And I know whose it is. Whose it *has* to be. Because on this night, it can belong to no other person.

Glenn wasn't working alone.

But a question remains: is Jack inside the car? Or is it someone else?

9

The car screeches to a halt. The door flings open.

Sarge gets out.

His gun is already pointed at us.

I can feel Dad's surprise. His dismay. His world tilting on an axis he always thought would be rock-solid. I can almost hear his thoughts: *Sarge, how could it be* Sarge? *Not Sarge!*

The guy who led them…

(*and was in a perfect position to pick the corrupt ones*)

… the guy who was the best of them…

(*and hid in plain sight because of it*)

… the guy who continually hounded them to make the next R&R bust…

(*and who just stole the drugs from evidence and re-dropped them in the Ocean's Tomb when it happened and so got the money for the drugs as well as the credit for the bust, a win-win*)

… the one Dad *trusted*.

Sarge's gun never waivers. And there's no chance of us getting the drop on him. None at all. He's the best of the cops. The best thinker, the best planner…

… the best shot.

"Why?" says Dad.

"It's nothing personal, Latham," says Sarge. He stays about fifteen feet away. Too close for him to miss a shot at, but too far for us to rush him. He knows what to do.

He's the best.

"I really hoped the night would turn out differently," he says.

"Me, too," says Dad.

They are quiet for a moment. Nearly a thoughtful time. Like old friends reunited and not sure what to say. Unsure how to begin, and unsure how they might have changed in the years that have passed.

"Well," Sarge finally says.

"Could you...." Dad's voice trails off. He laughs bitterly. "I don't suppose there's any chance you'd let Mel go?"

Sarge's gun actually falters a bit. He frowns. "Let her go?"

At that moment, Dad's radio activates. "Ah," whispers Jack. A quiet, "You're ready to see!"

Sarge takes no notice. He might as well not even have heard Jack speak. "Let her go?" he says again. "Latham, Mel's dead. She's been dead for a month."

PART SIX:
LAST CALL

June 30
PD Property Receipt – Evidence
Case # IA15-6-3086
Rec'd: 6/29
Investigating Unit: IA/Homicide

JOURNAL
DAY THIRTY

Short entry.

Dad's on his way to work.

I won't let him go without me.

1

Dad falls backward. A huge, lurching step that makes Sarge's words into more than sound. They are a physical attack. An attempted destruction of body, of mind... of self.

I don't move. I can't. I'm rooted to the spot.

"No," says Dad. His voice is a whisper. "She's not dead. She's... she's right here." He gestures at me.

Sarge frowns. Looks right at me. Shakes his head. "No, Latham. Sorry." He looks truly sad, disbelieving at the same time. "Is this what's been happening? Damn, I just thought you didn't want to be part of the deal anymore. Didn't know you'd just lost it."

"Deal?" I say.

(*or do I say it who is saying it who is speaking who –?*)

Another frown from Sarge. "But I kind of saw this coming. It's why I sent Ray and Bob to watch you. Just the way you screamed after I shot that dealer in the head – the asshole who tried to double cross us, who shot your daughter... the way you were screaming when the other guys took you from the alley. Screaming..."

... and as he says it, Dad's radio activates. Jack speaks in time. The voice from my dream. ""You killed my baby! I'll kill you! I'll kill you all!"

When Jack speaks, his voice shifts. The change is subtle, but by the time he screams "kill you all!" I finally recognize who he sounds like. The cadences, the patterns.

Jack sounds like my dad.

I fall back. Hit the Mustang.

It's no longer cold against my back.

Sarge takes no notice of Jack's voice. A voice that only sounds for me, for my dad. "We thought you might want to back out of the deal, even before we had to kill those dealers. But then your daughter happened along, ended up in the crossfire." He sighs. "I guess if you weren't already going to back out, it was a done deal after what happened to her." He smiles a shark-smile, all whites and killing hunger. "Bad day to buy a prom dress, huh?"

(*A beat cop's daughter doesn't shop on Rodeo Drive, doesn't even shop at Nordstrom. She shops where the deals are. And that's the garment district. I've been to the garment district for cheap jeans, for homecoming dresses. I was going to get my prom dress here, until things got weird with Liam and I didn't end up going.*)

[Why didn't I end up going? Why didn't I go to the prom with Liam?]

I can't remember. No matter how hard I try.

[Because I'm not here. I can't remember because I'm....]

"Dead," Dad says. He looks at Sarge. "You know Liam's dead, right?"

Sarge nods. "Yeah," he says. His voice emotionless. "He found out what we were into. I thought he'd be able to

229

handle it – it was all for him, after all. All for him to have a better future than a cop can afford. But then... Mel."

Dad shakes his head. Still denying. "No. No, he spoke to her. I heard her voice."

Jack's voice speaks from Dad's radio. And now I hear not only his voice, but Liam's. The voice of the dead, spoken as he died. And my voice comes out as well, as though Jack –

[who is he, who is Jack, what's HAPPENING?]

– had been there, recording it all.

("Liam," I say. "What happened?"

"YOU KNOW!" *he screams. Then whispers,* "You know." *Then, sobbing,* "I can't live without.... Mel, please talk to me."

Only this time I hear it differently. Not "I can't live without.... Mel, please talk to me," *but* "I can't live without Mel, please talk to me." *Speaking not to me, but to my* father. *To a man who will help – perhaps stop – his pain. The pain of losing his love, a month ago.)*

[Was I even there?]

In fact, now I think of it, no one has addressed me directly all night. No one has called me by name....

("I like these, too," says the lady at the Exxon food mart, pointing at the candy. "My favorite," I say.)

[Did I say it? Or did my father? Did Dad say it and only imagine it was me, only imagine there *was* a me?]

("I would've pegged you for..." she squints at me[/my father]. "Jerky. Peppered.")

230

[Peppered beef jerky. The kind of thing a big man, a cop, would eat.]

(*Ray, at Glenn's house, says, "You let 'em in, you dumbass?"*)

['Em. *Them.*

But could he have been saying, "You let *'im* in"? *Him*? Singular?]

(*What about the bartender? "Can I help you, Officer? Something to drink? Maybe something for your partner?"*)

[Who was he talking to? If not me, who was he talking to?]

(*And now I hear Sarge's voice. Saying, "Damn, I just thought you didn't want to be part of the deal anymore." Talking not just to my dad, not just to a cop... but to a fellow criminal.*)

[That's who he was talking to. The bartender was talking to my dad, and he knew what had happened because –

(*I suddenly wonder if there are dirty cops in this area.... Maybe Froggy's expecting a shakedown.*)

– he let the cops use his roof for the hit. He *knew*. And it was a subtle jab at Dad when he asked about "his partner," because he also knew Dad's partner was killed.]

[So what was *I* doing there that day?]

(*I remember earlier, when Liam called the morning of the ridealong: "I'm sorry about what happened. I'm so, so sorry."*]

[He was going to take me to prom. He thought it was his fault.]

(*In the alley, after he shot himself, Liam's last words: "You told me to come. Is this what you wanted?"*)

[No. That's not why I(/my dad?) wanted him there. I(/we) wanted to tell him what happened. What *really* happened. That it wasn't his fault. I was just shopping for a prom dress in a place I knew. In a place I knew because my father had taken me there. And in a place *he* knew, so he set up meets and drops there. Just like the cops all knew about the fish market, about Red Rocks, a perfect drop point where other cops would never look.]

I am starting to believe. Starting to lose myself.

[But I *did* things. I touched things.

Yes. So in sync with my father. All night. Knowing his thoughts. Fighting as one. Because there was only one person thinking, only one person fighting?]

(*Fighting with him, both of us moving as one.*)

(*Pulling the dumpster, each of us feeling like we were only pulling with half strength –*)

[Each of us only half a *person*?]

(*And when I climbed down into the Ocean's Tomb – the place where I killed a full-grown man with the strength and skill of a trained –*

[police officer]

– fighter? Underwater, batted around? And Dad lost his gun. We thought it was stolen by Jack.)

[But not stolen. It was simply lost. Simply lost in the surf under the Tomb. Because I was wearing it. In fact, the climb down was tight, because I was wearing a full rig, the ten extra pounds of a police belt around my waist. And after the dunking the radio didn't work, either. Dad[/I?]

232

couldn't call dispatch. Only Jack could use the radio. Only a phantom can use a broken thing.]

And Beardo?

(*Beardo: the man whose car we commandeered. So helpful-seeming. Until Dad mentions his sick passenger. Then… suspicion. Because what does he see in the empty space where Dad gestures? Not a sick passenger.*)

[He doesn't see *anything*.]

My mind scrabbles for last reasons this is wrong. Last rationales. Perhaps the last rites of a doomed soul.

(*What about my memories of Liam?*)

[All things Dad knew. Because he's known Liam as long as I have. He was there for most of them. I've told him the rest.]

[And my *injuries*?]

This is the final test. The ricochet so close it burns my neck, the bullet that notches my ear.

I feel neck. I feel ear.

Nothing. Whole flesh.

I look at Dad.

He has a burn mark on his neck. An ear that bleeds freely from a glancing bullet wound.

[What about Knight? Zevahk, Voss? If he's the one, then when did he…?]

And I remember. Remember sleeping the day away. Plenty of time for a man to set in motion a series of deaths and clues that will both exact revenge and hopefully bring him back to reality.

(*Voss's screams on the radio? "Please! PLEASE DON'T DO IT PLEASE JUST LET ME GO –"*)

[And now I think...

... think...

... no, more than thought. Memory...

... a man looming over Voss's crippled form.]

(*"You killed my daughter, Voss. We all did," says the man. And it sounds like Jack. Jack and another voice, more familiar.*

Then the man breaks the neck of the helpless Voss. Takes his body and drops it down the Tomb, then follows it in and secures it under the rocks. "Rot," says the man. "Rot in here. Rot in Hell."

He kills Knight. Stages the body in a way that will start this all. Because on some level the man knows this must end. He must wake himself up.

He breaks every bone in Zevahk's body. Stuffs him in a car to die, then takes the car to the beach before riding back to his cruiser in a taxi.

He gets in his cruiser.

I see his face.

Dad.)

[ME!]

So who am I? What am I? What is Mel? What is *ME*?

A ghost?

For a moment I think that must be it.

Then I realize. No ghost. I'm not a phantom. I'm less. I'm nothing. I'm...

... I'm madness.

I scream. And as I do, Jack's voice comes on the radio. Screaming. Sarge still does not hear that voice. Because he *cannot*.

Dad starts to scream, too.

We scream, but Sarge only hears Dad. Because I'm dead, and I'm nothing but imagination, and Jack is nothing but conscience, and then we're nothing but...

2

... me again. Back in my body, and fully awake for the first time since my daughter died.

The screams – my screams, Jack's screams, Mel's screams – bounce like bullets through my brain.

They killed her. The men I thought of as friends and brothers – they killed my daughter with their deals and their corruption and the fact that when the dealers tried to run they didn't let it just *happen*. More important to save the drugs than to save a life.

To save *Mel's* life.

She's gone. She's been gone the whole time. Just me. Just me talking to a no one, a ghost of my own making. Writing in a journal I always wished she would have kept, saying the words I wished she would say. Loving words, kind words.

Forgiving words.

I scream. Jack screams, because Jack is me – the best me, the part of me that is just a good father and never would have dreamed of being in that alley in the first place.

I scream. Then a shot sounds.

My scream ends, not with a whimper, but with a bang. I feel the bullet hit me in the chest. Dead center.

Sarge is a good shot.

But he missed my heart. I was twisting during my shrieking. It saved my life.

Jack speaks. He speaks from the dead and from a broken radio and from the nothing of my mind.

"End it," he says. His voice is mine.

I raise my gun. The gun I took from Ray.

Sarge pulls the trigger of his gun again. His second bullet takes me in the shoulder.

I don't care.

Sarge is the best of us.

But I've always been a decent shot. Maybe not the best, but good enough.

Good enough for this.

I pull my own trigger.

The shot opens him up. Slams him against his cruiser and to the ground, looking at me through three eyes instead of two.

A moment later I fall as well. Leaning against the Mustang. It's cool, just like I remember. Just like when I was Mel.

Jack whispers to me. The voice no longer in my radio, but in my own mind.

"It's over. You did it. You killed them all." He sounds fully and completely like me. At last. "It's over," he says again.

"Yeah," I say back.

I know I'm crazy. I know I've been crazy for weeks.

But it doesn't matter. I ended it. I ended it all. Killed the ones who killed my baby girl.

My job's done. Everything's done.

I feel a hand on mine.

I look up.

Mel is there. She's smiling at me.

She's wearing a prom dress. And I think... I think maybe Liam is standing behind her. They look great together.

(*They're not really here.*)

(*I don't care.*)

"Hey, Melly Belly," I say.

"I hate when you call me that," she says.

"Sorry," I say. Even though we both know I'm really not. She'll always be Melly Belly to me.

She pulls my hand. I stand up. Light as a feather, and free as a bird.

"Come on," she says. "It's time for me to take *you* on a ride."

I smile. "That sounds nice," I say.

FOR READERS:
You can sign up for Michaelbrent's newsletter, with giveaways and the latest releases, at <u>writteninsomnia.com/michaelbrents-minions</u>
and get a free book for signing up!
*

A REQUEST FROM THE AUTHOR:
If you loved this book and have a moment to spare, **I would really appreciate a short review on the page where you bought the book**. Your help in spreading the word is more appreciated than I can say, and the reviews make a **huge** difference in helping new readers find my books. And that matters, since that's how I keep writing and (more important) take care of my family.

\-   Michaelbrent

*

FOR WRITERS:
Michaelbrent has helped hundreds of people write, publish, and market their books through articles, audio, video, and online courses. For his online courses, check out
<u>http://michaelbrentcollings.thinkific.com</u>
*

ABOUT THE AUTHOR
Michaelbrent is an internationally-bestselling author, produced screenwriter, and member of the Writers Guild of America, but his greatest jobs are being a husband and father. See a complete list of Michaelbrent's books
at <u>writteninsomnia.com</u>.

FOLLOW MICHAELBRENT
Twitter: <u>twitter.com/mbcollings</u>
Facebook: <u>facebook.com/MichaelbrentCollings</u>

Made in United States
North Haven, CT
23 January 2025

64809362R00152